Praise for Gregory Mcdonald's
Son of Fletch:

"Sheer pleasure." —Peter Straub

"The dialogue is fast, funny and fearfully clever . . . better than most crime fiction out there . . . a heck of a lot of fun." —Trenton *Times*

"Readers will gladly succumb to Mcdonald's laconic wit and smooth pacing . . . Fletch, Carrie, and the enterprising Jack . . . are all fully dimensioned characters who rate readers' attention and applause." —*Publishers Weekly*

"He certainly hasn't forgotten how to leap right into a story . . . Jack seems like a chip off the old block."
—*The Washington Post*

"I adored *Son of Fletch*." —Lia Matera

"Health warning to mystery readers: *Son of Fletch* stopped me from sleeping last night. It must be the wittiest, twistiest story I've read this year, and consequently very addictive." —Peter Lovesey

FLETCH
REFLECTED

GREGORY
MCDONALD

J

JOVE BOOKS, NEW YORK

This Jove Book contains the complete text of the original hardcover edition. It has been completely reset in a typeface designed for easy reading and was printed from new film.

FLETCH REFLECTED

A Jove Book / published by arrangement with the author

PRINTING HISTORY
G. P. Putnam's Sons edition published September 1994
Jove edition / August 1995

ISBN: 0-515-11676-9

A JOVE BOOK®
Jove Books are published by The Berkley Publishing Group, 200 Madison Avenue, New York, New York 10016.
JOVE and the "J" design are trademarks belonging to Jove Publications, Inc.

PRINTED IN THE UNITED STATES OF AMERICA

10 9 8 7 6 5 4 3

FLETCH
REFLECTED

1

"**F**aoni." In fact, he was answering the telephone at Andy Cyst's desk in the huge Global Cable News building in Virginia. He had no desk, or telephone, of his own.

The switchboard knew he was working with Andy Cyst.

"Fletch?"

"Who is this?"

The young woman's voice said, "Is this Fletch?"

"Yeah. Jack. Faoni. Fletch."

"I know your name is Jack Faoni. The weekend we spent together you had me call you Fletch."

"When was that?"

"Skiing. In Stowe, Vermont. A few years ago. We met there. At The Shed. You were with some other guys from a lumber camp. Playing your guitar. People were buying you beer to keep you playing. Well, I sort of kidnapped you. First, I kidnapped your guitar." Her voice was low, and warm. "When you pursued me to the parking lot to get your guitar back, I grabbed you. It was snowing. You were very hot. I ripped your shirt. I pulled it down off your shoulders. Do you remember the snowflakes falling on your sweating shoulders while we kissed? You sizzled."

"Good grief! Whoever you are, woman, you just elevated my temperature by more than a little. I'm hot now." Sticking a finger inside his shirt collar, Jack scanned the huge, brightly lit, colorful, air-conditioned room filled with journalists' workstations. "I wasn't a minute ago."

"You were very playful. Silly. You don't remember me?"

"I do." She had coal black hair, very wide-set coal-black eyes . . . And her name was? "I remember you weren't there when I woke up."

"I had to meet my father early for Belgian waffles. It really wasn't a weekend we spent together. Just a few lovely hours."

"I remember it was a cold morning and I had to run through the snow in a flannel shirt torn to shreds. Thanks for leaving me my guitar, anyway."

"You use your hands beautifully."

"Why didn't you come back? Leave a note? Something?"

"I had to ski with my father. Then he drove me back to Poughkeepsie."

"I waited." He had not waited long. The snow was pure powder, the skiing too good to miss. "I wasn't sure you weren't a dream."

"Anyway, I've been seeing your name on GCN the last few days. Those great stories about the Tribe."

"Thanks. I guess."

"You're working for GCN now?"

"I guess so. I'm here. They've used everything I've brought them."

"That's great. But they never showed your face on television. If it was your story, why didn't they use you on camera?"

"One doesn't do that."

"One doesn't? A lot do."

"People come to recognize you. Then you can't do the kind of stories I want to do."

"Oh. You must have been working on that story a long time."

"It took a long time to set up. Once it got going, it went quickly. Very quickly."

"So guess where I am."

"You like games, don't you?"

"Yeah. I do."

"Let me think . . . You're in jail?"

"No."

"You're in hospital with some horrible disease the doctor says you must tell me about?"

"No."

"I give up." Jack rearranged some papers on Andy Cyst's desk. "Why don't you remind me of your name, if you ever shared it with me in the first place, tell me where you are, if that's relevant to the conversation, then tell me why you called.

You've talked so long I'm beginning to need a shower."

"We didn't do all that much talking, as I remember. We went at each other like bear cubs."

"I don't care who you are. I don't care where you are. I don't care why you're calling. Goodbye."

"Staufel."

"Is that a name, or an order?"

"Shana Staufel."

"Oh, yes. Shana. So where are you, Shana?"

"Vindemia."

"Vindemia. I've read that word somewhere. What is it, defunct coal mines in Appalachia, what?"

"One of the biggest estates in America."

"Oh, yeah. In Georgia? Owned by . . ."

"Actually, I'm calling you from a phone booth outside the Vindemia Gas Station and General Store. The estate has its own little village, complete with chapel, library, and many, many rent-a-cops."

"Cute. Owned by . . . the guy who invented uh . . ."

"Chester Radliegh. He invented the perfect mirror."

"Oh, yeah. The guy who straightened out our left from our right, right from left when we look at ourselves in a mirror."

"Right. Chester Radliegh. Massive implications for industry, science, space . . ."

"You sound like you're quoting from *Business Digest.*"

"I am. I looked him up. Before I met him."

"Boxers appreciate his mirror, too."

"They do?"

"They don't get blindsided so much these days. Haven't you noticed?"

"Guess I haven't."

"More fights go the whole ten, fifteen rounds now."

"Is that good?"

"Think of the philosophical, psychological, to say nothing of poetic ramifications of the perfect mirror. I mean, for centuries we were seeing ourselves wrong, weren't we? Not as others saw us, as they say."

"Do we ever, anyway?"

"I'd like to meet him. Radliegh must have an interesting mind. To take a thing as ancient and simple as the mirror and realize it was wrong; it was backward . . . 'In the clear mirror of thy ruling star/ I saw, alas!, some dread event depend.' "

"Who said that?"

"Before I did? A guy named Pope."

"I'm going to marry Chet."

"What's a Chet?"

"Chester Radliegh, Jr."

"Oh. You called to invite me to your wedding? I'll send a present. Shreds of my flannel shirt, as a keepsake, or a dustcloth, whichever you need the more."

"Not exactly."

"What then?"

"To invite you here."

"Where? Vindemia?"

"Yes."

"You need someone to speak up for you? A play-mate reference, maybe?"

"This is the first time I've ever been here. I've come to meet the family."

"I don't get it. Why would you need me? Even want me in the same state?"

"You're an investigative reporter."

"Thanks."

"There's something real weird about this place. These people."

"Sure. They got very, very rich, very, very fast. Who said, 'Wealth doesn't corrupt as much as it reveals'?"

"Pope?"

"I don't think so."

"I want you to come here. I can say you're my cousin."

"As I remember, we look nothing alike."

"Sometimes cousins don't. You could just be passing by and drop in for a few days."

"Sure. You're marrying into a maxi-wealthy family, get brought home by Chet ditto to meet Mama, Papa and the Borzoi hound, and your distant relatives start landing on them asking directions to their larder. What kind of an impression would that make?"

"This place is so big, there are so many people wandering around, you wouldn't even be noticed."

"Yeah, I do a pretty good imitation of a potted palm. You telling me you think there's a story for me here somewhere? What is it? The guy's been profiled a million times. A Massachusetts Institute of Technology professor of physics invents the perfect mirror, makes zillions of dollars between a Tuesday and Friday, buys half the state of Georgia, builds a fifty room mansion—"

"Seventy two. Seventy two rooms."

"Really? I thought I was exaggerating."

"The roof is five acres."

"Lor' love a duck! I've been on farms smaller than that."

"Five acres, they tell me. It looks it."

"—has a gorgeous, well-behaved family—"

"That's where the profile goes awry."

"They are not a gorgeous, well-behaved family?"

"They're gorgeous." She hesitated.

"So?"

"I think they want to kill him."

"What? Who?"

"Chester Radliegh. I think his family wants to murder him. His friends. The people who work for him. Everybody around him. I'm afraid one of them will succeed."

"What on earth makes you say a thing like that? Is he that much of a bastard?"

"He's a wonderful man."

"Then why do you say such a thing?"

"I don't know, exactly. Things are weird here. Little things. Everything is so tight, you know? Security. Yet, these weird little things keep happening. I think Chester, Mister Radliegh, thinks he has invented the perfect mirror in his family, all the people he has collected around him, except they're not perfect, they seem to want to leap at him. . . ."

Andy Cyst was walking from the administration offices toward his desk. The room was so big Jack thought there was a need for conveyer belts on the floor. It was not a city room; it was a world room; a cosmic room.

Jack took his feet off the edge of Andy's console desk.

". . . That's why I want you to come here," Shana continued. "Investigate this. There's so much tension. I'm afraid of what's going to happen."

Jack stretched the muscles of his upper back. He had had an exciting but exhausting few weeks. "Well, I'd like to meet Mister Radliegh, as I said," Jack said into the phone, "but I do have a job, I think, and you understand I can't drop everything and come to some Valhalla in the sky, pass myself off as some itinerant relation to the daughter-in-law to be, just in case the butler spits in Daddy's mock turtle soup. You do understand that, don't you?"

"What can I do to persuade you?"

"Make me believe there's a story here."

"Is 'story' all that matters to you? I've heard you

play the guitar. I've had you in bed. The whole world has just seen this wonderful exposé of the Tribe you've done. You mean to tell me you don't care about people?"

"Get some evidence. Find me a plan to collapse those five acres of roof on Chester Radliegh."

"I was hoping you'd do that. Find evidence, I mean."

"I have a life, lady."

"Lucky you."

"Give me your phone number, just in case old Chester gets carted off to the hospital with a case of botulism, or something."

She recited the main number of the estate. "There's a switchboard," she said. "I'm in the American Girl Rose Suite."

Andy stepped into his workstation.

"What does that mean?" Jack asked.

"The suites don't have numbers. Each is named after a particular flower, or plant. My suite is called the American Girl Rose Suite."

"Ah. I see. Sounds homey enough. Does it come complete with pricks?"

"Homey enough if your last name is Windsor. Will you at least think about it?"

"I don't see how I can."

Shana Staufel sighed. "Okay. Well, it was nice meeting you. Nice talking to you."

"Best wishes," Jack said, "on your marriage."

• • •

"A story?" Andy asked.

"A girl."

Jack stood up.

"Alex Blair asked me to tell you to come to his office right away."

"Who's he?"

"His office is down the Central Corridor, right next to the C.E.O.'s." Andy sat in his chair. "He's waiting for you now."

"Okay."

"Jack?"

"Yeah?"

"You know, one of my assignments here is to answer the phone to Mister Fletcher. He's a stockholder. A director. He has a past in this business, at least print journalism, I don't know, was a respected journalist, I guess: I've heard he was; I've heard he wasn't. Sometimes he calls me three and four times a day. Then weeks will go by when I don't hear from him at all. When he has story ideas, needs some research done."

"Sounds like a tough assignment."

"No," Andy said. "It's interesting. I try to figure out what he's doing, thinking, what he's working on by the questions he asks. He's very oblique. Almost never do his questions mean nothing. Usually something interesting results; sometimes something sensational. I'm learning a lot from him. I think I am. It was that way regarding the Tribe story. There were little questions about the Tribe I could have ignored, about a jailbreak in Kentucky, about a woman named Faoni. One huge story developed, and one very good story."

"This guy Blair is waiting for me."

"How did you meet Mister Fletcher, Jack? How did your paths cross?"

Jack said, "Ask him."

2

"**J**ack!" Rising from behind his massive mahogany desk, the slim, graying man in the form fitting blue suit seemed genuinely glad to see him. Smiling, he came around the desk and shook Jack's hand with both of his. "I've been seeing you around the office all week, of course, but I haven't had the chance to stop and say hello."

His gray eyes were not smiling.

"Are you Mister Blair?" The smiling secretary had nodded Jack through the office door without speaking.

"Alex." The man continued to hold Jack's hand. "Call me Alex."

Returning to his desk, Blair nearly sang, "What a wonderful story! So glad to nail those racist bastards! Wish we could rid the world of that scum for all time! We're so damned pleased you brought the story to Global Cable News!" He sat in the tall leather swivel chair behind his desk. "Sit down, Jack, sit down!"

Sitting, Jack looked around the office. All the wood was mahogany, or appeared to be. Everything else Jack had seen in the GCN building was glass, steel, plastic—very good plastic, of course. In the mahogany bookcases were television screens, rows of them.

"So," Jack said, "you're the guy who fixes the t.v.'s?"

"What?" Blair followed Jack's eyes to the rows of t.v. sets. "Oh!" He chuckled. "A little joke."

Jack smiled his agreement with Blair's assessment.

Blair stirred some papers around on the glass surface of his desk. "We need your Social Security number."

Jack reached for his wallet. "I thought you'd never ask. Where are you going to assign me?"

"Where what?" The man kept his eyes on his desk.

"I'm free to take a foreign assignment," Jack said. "Not married. Not entangled."

"We have your name as John Faoni." He spelled Faoni. "Have we been right about that?"

"Yes," Jack answered. "J-O-H-N."

"You know, we don't even have your address."

"I don't have one here in Washington, yet. Will I need one? You've been putting me up in a motel down the highway."

"Oh, yes. Is it comfortable?"

"I don't know. I've been spending day and night in this building, getting these stories out. This is the first morning I've had nothing to do."

"I had lunch in that motel once."

"Was it good?"

Blair's cheeks colored slightly. "Brunch, actually."

"Oh," Jack said. "You slept late."

Jack handed his Social Security card to Blair and recited his mother's address in Indiana.

Blair asked, "How did you happen to come across Mister Fletcher?" At Jack's lack of response, Blair continued. "Very fortunate for us you did. Mister Fletcher is a great friend to all of us here at GCN. On the Board of Directors, a Consulting/Contributing Editor, but working as he does in his own unorthodox ways, well outside, away from the network, he brings great freshness to us. Keeps us honest, in some ways. However it happened, you were very lucky to cross paths with him."

"Yes," Jack said. "Lucky."

"He worked with you on the Tribe stories, yet accepted no credit for them."

Jack said nothing.

"What did you say your relationship is with Mister Fletcher?"

"Relationship?" Jack would be damned before he would state his "relationship" with the member of the Board of Directors of Global Cable News, Consulting/Contributing Editor Irwin Maurice Fletcher.

He would be damned if he would tell every turkey who gobbled, especially one who could influence his career positively, that the above described Irwin Maurice Fletcher was the real and natural father he had always heard about, read about, read, dreamed about . . .

And that Jack had arranged to meet for the first time ever only the week before . . .

That the Tribe exposé was Jack's story . . .

And that Jack had gone well out of his way to suck the aforesaid Fletcher senior reluctantly into the investigation of the story, to see what his father was really like . . .

And so that his father could see what he, Jack, was really like.

Not his style.

"Yes. I mean, we're puzzled as to why he gave you these stories on the Tribe, worked with you, then sent you to us. Why didn't he use our own people?"

"This was my story," Jack said. "I set it up. Mister Fletcher didn't become involved until nearly the end of the investigation."

"So." Blair smiled knowingly. "You involved him in it so you could have access to Global Cable News."

Jack said nothing.

"Very generous of him," Blair insisted. "Typical of him, I must say."

Blair handed a thick, folded paper across the desk to Jack. "Lucky for us," Blair said. "Lucky for you.

I couldn't stand the sight of those people, myself."

Jack unfolded the paper. It was a check drawn on a Global Cable News bank account for a large sum of money. It was made out to John Faoni.

"That's nice," Jack said.

"Commensurate with our appreciation," Blair said. "Your stories on the Tribe made quite an international splash. Shouldn't be surprised if they won us some prizes."

"Let's hope," Jack said. He was puzzled by the large amount of the check. "So . . . I get one of these every week?"

"Pardon?"

"What, what . . ." First, Jack had asked what his assignment would be, and had had no answer. "Just what will my annual salary be?"

"From . . . ?" Blair let the preposition hang in the air.

Jack realized he had let a proposition hang in the air. A presumption. "Global Cable News."

"You're not an employee of Global Cable News, Mister Faoni."

"But . . ."

"We looked at your work as a favor to Mister Fletcher. It just happened to work out. This time."

"You're not offering me a job?"

"Of course not. We don't even know you. You arrived here looking like something washed up on the beach, carrying a sack of videotapes and computer disks, which we were able to use. I understand we had only one phone call from Mister

Fletcher. If we hadn't had that, you never would have gotten in the door."

"I had the story!"

"And we gave you credit. And"—Blair's gray eyes looked at the check in Jack's hand—"payment."

Jack looked down at the check. "You're paying me off?"

"With thanks. Didn't Andy tell me you're still in journalism school somewhere?"

"I can't go back there. Not at this point."

"Well, wait till the term rolls 'round again. You have the money in your hands for a nice vacation. My wife and I are very fond of taking the train trip across Canada. Magnificent scenery. Excellent service."

"You're not offering me a job?"

"Things are tight here now, Jack. There's so much competition in this business. We have difficulty, you see, in persuading all American businesses they should spend as much as eighty percent of their gross income on advertising. A few still resist the idea. We're not exactly laying people off, but we are not replacing people who leave for one reason or another. What we need are young people with experience. Just because you've worked on one story we do not consider you experienced."

"It was my story. My name was on it. It was a great story. You said it should be a prizewinner."

"Yes." Blair smiled. "We're very grateful to Mister Fletcher."

Jack tightened his jaw. He was sorely tempted . . .

He had to remind himself of what was his style, and what wasn't.

"Naturally," Blair said softly, "we hope that if you ever come across another story like the Tribe you'll talk to us about it first. Maybe a little earlier in the investigation of the story. . . . We have more experienced people here. I mean, that story really should have been a team effort."

" 'A team effort'?" Jack could not imagine a t.v. film crew swarming the Tribe's encampment and getting much of a story. That wouldn't have been journalism; that would have been publicity.

"We would have liked to have vetted some of the things you undoubtedly did to get that story with our legal department, for example. We can only hope that legal repercussions won't develop from your work. I'm advised there are certain concerns that might be raised regarding privacy issues."

"You're worried about being sued by White Supremacists for my invading their privacy?"

"You were on private land. The computer system you broke into . . ."

"Lor' love a duck," Jack said. "You television wallahs just want pictures."

"And of course you started the story while you were in prison, didn't you?"

"You don't understand that? I was placed in the prison—"

"I know what I've heard. One never knows what's true."

"One doesn't?" Jack's mouth was dry. "Isn't that what this business is about?"

"Oh, sure." Blair's smile was sardonic. "That's what I mean, Jack. You need experience. Go back to school. Go somewhere you can do lots of stories. Develop a first class résumé. Right now . . . left school . . . prison . . . white supremacists . . . who knows what you are . . . a diamond in the rough, maybe . . ."

Check in hand, Jack rose from his chair.

"It's been nice meeting you, Mister Blair." He reached his arm across the mahogany desk. Blair rose and shook Jack's hand.

"Hope you don't mind my giving you a little fatherly advice," Blair said. "You got credit for this big story, but it's ours now. We bought it. It's over. And essentially you are untried. You lucked out, once. This is over. It's a big, dirty world out there, no one owes you a living, go back to school, get a job, get married, have kids, who knows, you might be happy in some other line of work altogether. . . ."

Still holding Blair's hand, staring into his gray eyes, Jack said, "Sorry you fell overboard. My door is always closed to you."

"What?" Uncertainly, Blair chuckled.

Jack said, "Bye."

3

"**V**indemia. Good morning. How may I help you?"

"Will you ring the American Girl Rose Suite, please?" Jack asked.

"Ringing."

Again, Jack was using Andy Cyst's phone.

"No answer, sir, in the American Girl Rose Suite."

"I'm calling for Ms. Shana Staufel."

"I doubt Ms. Staufel would be in her room at 11:30 in the morning, sir. Hold on." Jack held on. At the moment he didn't much care what this personal telephone call cost Global Cable News. "Sir? I've tried the outdoor pool, the spa, the skeet-shooting range, the golf house, and the stables. Is there anywhere else you think I should try?"

"Yeah. The phone outside the gas station in the village."

"Sorry, sir. That's a pay phone. We can't plug into that."

"May I leave a message?"

"Certainly, sir."

"This is Jack Faoni. The message is, 'Prepare the Cactus Suite, Coz.' "

"Fletch. Hello?"

"Hey, Dad."

"Urmph."

"What's the matter?"

"Nothing. Something made my ears block." Fletch wondered if he'd ever get used to the word "Dad." There must be some alternative. The young man so enjoyed using it.

Until a week before, Fletch had never known he had a son.

He still hadn't taken legal advice to prove that one John Fletcher Faoni was his son.

"Where are you?" Jack asked.

"Approaching Forward, Wisconsin, from the southeast."

"I'm surprised you dare show your face in that burg."

"Thought I'd better clean up the mess I helped make for your mother. Today is moving day for the denizens of Blythe Spirit."

"Your story on GCN closed down Mama's favorite fat farm?"

"As a journalist, never be the rooster who believes it is only his crowing which brings up the sun."

"Now what will she do?"

"The State of Wisconsin is closing it down, for health reasons, while handing out fraud indictments to everyone involved they can find."

"Are you going to pick her up?"

"Is that a joke?"

"You can't pick up a woman who weighs over six hundred pounds? Mama done tol' me you were always pickin' up all kindsa wimmin."

"I am driving a rented handicap van with a hydraulic lift."

"She'll be furious with you. Blythe Spirit has become her home away from home."

"And her major expense. A lot of good it was doing her. Did you know the staff at Blythe Spirit had pretty well convinced your mother she must plan to spend the rest of her life with them?"

"Oh, no."

"Oh, yes. With one hand they fed her appetites, with the other hand they fed her despair, while somehow continuing to pick her pockets. For a bright woman such as your mother, that took real sleight of hand."

"It's okay, Dad. As her son, I can tell you she might take a swing at you, but she can't catch you. Just don't ever let her fall on you."

Fletch said, "You mean, again."

"Again?"

"Look what happened last time she fell on me."

"Yeah," Jack said. "I happened. Aren't you glad?"

"We'll see."

"Sure you are."

"Now I know why you're so nimble footed."

"Live with a six hundred plus pound mama for a while," Jack said, "and you learn to take short, rapid, circuitous steps. Dos yee doe."

"So how are you doing, Nijinski?"

"Who's Nijinski?" Jack asked.

"Someone who could dance around women pretty well, too."

"I'm fine," Jack answered. "The stories exposing the Tribe made a big splash around the whole world. Or so I'm told. Did you see any of the stories on GCN?"

"You know we don't have cable at the farm. But I've been reading about your stories in the press. I'm proud of you. You didn't do any on-camera work, did you?"

"What do you mean?"

"They didn't show you, pictures of you, did they?"

"No. They wanted to, bad enough. In the vein of Young Reporter Risks Himself. I didn't let them. Some of your principles have gotten through to me, you know."

"Oh. Your mama taught you well."

"But gee, Dad, it really crimps the vanity, you know? I coulda been a see-leb-pretty."

"I'm sure. As the preacher said to his daughter,

'Save yourself. There's always tomorrow.' "

"Yeah. I had a date with her once. Speaking of people who don't put out, I just met your Mr. Blair."

"Alex Blair? He's a jerk."

"Gee, Dad, and I thought he was real nice."

"I'm sure you did."

"Such a sincere man."

"As sincere as a snake on a rock stirrin' his tail in the water."

"He gave me a nice big check."

"I see." Driving through rural Wisconsin, Fletch was trying to find a roadsign for the town of Forward. "That means GCN didn't offer you a job."

"It's a very generous check."

"Bastards. Which also means you didn't let them know you're my son." In the van by himself, Fletch smiled. "Isn't that right?"

"Gee, Dad, am I your son?"

"Until further notice."

"You're not going to make me submit to DNA tests?" Jack asked.

"I hate the question. I don't even know why you'd want to be my son. Your mother raised you, filling you up with all kinds of lies about me. . . . All I've ever done is write a book you don't like much."

"Well, I look at it this way," Jack said. "You still have an opportunity to turn out well. Just maybe, with my good influence on you—"

"You intend to reform me at this point? Good luck."

"Hey, I might even teach you one or two things about journalism."

"What are you going to do now that GCN has given you your walking papers?"

"Visit an old girlfriend in Georgia."

"How close an old girlfriend?"

"She's getting married. To someone else."

"The best kind."

"We only spent a very short weekend together once. Very short."

"I've got the picture. You were at the Heartbreak Motel. So why are you showing up in her life now that she's getting married? Can't you stand any rejection at all?"

"She's invited me. She thinks there's something weird about her boyfriend's family."

"Isn't there always? Few are the brides who realize it in time. You're investigating the in-laws for her?"

"Something like that."

"Why? Doesn't sound like there's a story there."

"Does there always have to be a story?"

"You've got to keep yourself in Pepsi and pizza, boy."

"You haven't asked me who her in-laws are."

"Who?"

"Professor and Mrs. Chester Radliegh."

"Oh, yes. I see. He who invented the perfect

mirror. Georgia. Isn't he the guy that built that crazy place . . . ?"

"Vindemia. That's where I'm going."

"I see. I guess I wouldn't mind meeting the guy who invented the wheel."

" 'To collect characters for the long ride,' " Jack quoted. "Isn't that what I'm supposed to say at this point?"

"Jeez, kid, you're stealing all my best lines."

"It might be interesting, don't you think? For some reason Shana thinks the Professor's life is in danger."

"If it doesn't work out, come back to Priory Farm, will you? Carrie insists she likes you and wouldn't mind having you around for a while. Besides, the fences always need painting. We can offer you minimum wage, a shed to sleep in, and a bath on Saturdays."

"Naw," Jack said. "As a father and son, we've grown too close."

"Sure," Fletch said. "I've seen you two or three times now, spent hours with you."

"It's not the quantity of time we spend together, it's the quality."

"Well . . ." Fletch spotted the sign for Forward and slowed the van for a left turn. "You sure got my attention the few days we spent together."

"How is Carrie?"

"Didn't I just say? She's crazy. She likes you. She loves me."

"Just wanted you to know where I'll be," Jack

said. "Tell my mother, please."

"Sure," Fletch said, turning the van left at the intersection. "Call if you find work."

"Want to go have lunch?" Andy Cyst asked.

"Yeah," John Fletcher Faoni answered.

"We might as well go to the employees' dining room. Lasagna is the special today."

"No," Jack said, "I want an Italian submarine sandwich."

"Where are you going to get that?"

"Subs Rosa."

"Where's that?"

"North Carolina."

"Uh?"

Jack shook Andy's hand. "It's been fun. Thanks for all your help."

"Blair didn't give you a job?"

"He gave me what he called 'fatherly advice,' to wit: get lost."

"Hey, Jack!" Andy called after him. "Will I see you again?"

Walking toward the exit of Global Cable News, Jack turned and waved at Andy.

Jack sang, "Maybe when I learn not to end a sentence with a proposition."

4

"**T**ell me who the bastard is now," Crystal demanded through clenched jaws at the sight of Fletch.

She was lying on the big bed in what had been her room on the second floor of Blythe Spirit. There were no pillowcases, sheets, blankets on the bed. There was no curtain around the bed.

She was an enormous mound of mostly useless flesh in an outsized nightgown and bathrobe.

To Fletch she looked as helpless, vulnerable as someone lying in the middle of a highway after a car wreck.

Except through a curtain the week before, Fletch had not seen Crystal in years. When he had entered the room he was physically shocked by her mammoth size.

Fletch exhaled. "Hi."

"They've even taken the lamps," Crystal said. "The reading lamps."

"Yeah. This is a busy old place today." There were cars, station wagons, ambulances, trucks, some of them with official insignias on their doors, crammed in Blythe Spirit's horseshoe driveway. Files were being wheeled out of the administration offices downstairs on dollies. He cleared his throat. "Let me take you away from all this."

"I'm not going anywhere with you," Crystal snapped. "You put the law on us. Your damned report on Global Cable News."

"You know I'm right."

"I know no such thing. These people were taking care of me."

"These people were keeping you handicapped so they could pick your pockets."

"Where's Jack?"

"Virginia. I was just talking to him."

"Is he coming?"

"No. He's on his way to Georgia."

"What did he say to you?"

Fletch smiled. "He told me to be careful not to let you fall on me again."

After looking at Fletch a moment from the bed, Crystal laughed. "This time, I'd crush you to death."

"Flatter than a manhole cover."

"You're both bastards. Father and son. I shouldn't have let one of you know the other existed. Get out of here. Who needs you?"

"You do."

"I don't."

"Okay. What are your plans?"

On her bed, Crystal raised her arm and dropped it in an impatient gesture. Watching her, Fletch realized the woman was so fat she probably could not sit up without help. "You have no responsibility for me," she muttered.

"I know." Softly, Fletch said, "But I told you Sunday I'd be back."

He continued to stand halfway between the bed and the door to the hall.

"Yeah," Crystal said. "You sneak in here as a reporter, spy on me, spy on the people taking care of me, blow the story on Global Cable News, cause every law enforcement agency, health agency, and tin-whistle politician to lay siege to this place, get everybody from the cook to the secretary in the office indicted, get the place closed down in hours, and here I am, stranded on this bed, unable to move, with nothing to eat all morning, I might add, without even a tissue to throw at you! You came back, all right. You're back like the second half of a hurricane on a seaside resort!"

Fletch grinned. "Haven't lost your fight, anyway."

"Why didn't Jack come?"

"Oh, I suspect he's giving us a chance to get reacquainted."

"You don't want to know me."

"Maybe not."

"I'm a mess."

"You're in a mess."

"It's not your fault."

"Who's talking about fault?"

"You didn't neglect me. You didn't know I had a son by you. I purposely dropped out of your sight so I could raise him myself."

"I know."

"I didn't need you then, and I don't need you now."

"You needed me once. A little bit. For a few minutes."

"I don't blame you for hating me. Doing this to me. Wrecking Blythe Spirit with a stroke of your coaxial sword. You always know how to get back at people, don't you, Fletch?"

"I'm not getting back at you."

"Of course you are. You found out about our son, Jack, that I had him and kept him from you and in four days I'm lying here stranded, starving, mortified beyond belief."

"That's okay," he said, "as long as you're not indulging in self-pity."

From the bed, she shot him a glance and half a smile. She said, "I'll bet you've even had breakfast."

"On the plane to Chicago," he said. "A coffee and muffin."

"Coffee and muffin!" she scoffed. "What kind of a muffin?"

"Blueberry."

"Call that breakfast?"

"Actually, no," Fletch answered. "What I might call breakfast would be, let me see, a half a fresh, chilled grapefruit, eggs scrambled with cream cheese, a steak, medium rare, a few sticks of crisp bacon, home-fried potatoes, maybe just a slice or two of summer sausage with fresh lemon juice—"

"Shut up."

"—buttered toast with, let's see, strawberry preserves would be nice—"

Crystal's eyes were full on him. "You eat all that stuff? For breakfast?"

"Are you going to get off that bed?"

"I can't! Can't you see?"

"I can see an enormously fat person, lying on a bed in a fraudulent medical facility rapidly being closed by the authorities, whose sheets, blankets, reading lamp and tissue box have been taken from her, who hints to me she is hungry, but who isn't doing anything about her situation. Are you going to die there, Crystal? One thing I absolutely will not do for you is serve as your pallbearer. We'll have to plant you with a crane."

"I have done something about it."

"What have you done? Sent out for Chinese?"

"You're killing me."

"You're killing yourself. What have you done to save yourself?"

"There's an ambulance coming for me."

"You sent for it?"

"No."

"An ambulance to take you where?"

"To the public hospital."

"Crystal, the public cannot afford you. Not you

and schools and the police and fire departments, too."

"They'll probably put me in the psychiatric ward." She sniffed.

Her head was turned toward the window. "I can't afford myself."

"Probably not."

"I don't need you."

"Okay."

"I don't need you. I don't need Jack. I don't need anybody."

Fletch sighed. "Crystal, when I left here Sunday, I said I'd be back. I'm back. If I leave here again, I won't be back."

"Go."

"I'll never enter this room again."

"So go."

Fletch said, "Okay."

He left.

"Mortimer."

"Hi, Mister Mortimer. This is Fletch."

"Who?"

"I. M. Fletcher."

"Oh, no."

"Did I call you at a bad time?"

"Yeah. I am not dead yet."

"How have you been otherwise?" Fletch was using the phone in the handicap van. He had not left the front driveway of Blythe Spirit.

"Well enough to hang up on you."

"Oh, don't do that."

"Why not?"

"I might have something interesting to say."

"You always do. That's why I'm hanging up. I'm too old to be interested in anything you have to say."

"Come on, now."

"Last time I listened to you is how I got so old. I was a young man, until then, with a full head of hair, a straight back, and friends. I listened to you and my hair grayed and fell out, my gums sank, my back stooped, my skin wrinkled, I lost my way of making a living, I lost all my friends—all in the three months I listened to you. I should listen to you again?"

"This time you might find it rejuvenating."

"Sure. This time I'll end up wearing incontinence pads."

"Hey, I—"

"No 'Hey, I—' nothing, Fletcher! You talked me into turning state's evidence. Everybody else, all my friends in the business went to jail. I was sent to Wyoming, for my own protection, ha! I'd rather be in jail. I would have known what I was doing in jail. What am I doing in Wyoming? There would have been more people I know in jail. We would have had a lot to talk about. I don't know anybody in Wyoming. All the people here talk about is something they call beef cattle and the twelve deadly sins."

"Seven."

"Seven what?"

"I think it's considered there are only seven deadly sins."

"In Wyoming, they got twelve."

"It is a big state."

"I can't figure out whether Wyoming is big or just empty."

"Mister Mortimer, you turned state's evidence after your best crack at a world middleweight championship got impaled on an iron railing in Gramercy Park."

"I did take that hard, yes. I loved that boy."

"You can write letters to your friends you put in jail."

"I do. A few of them. The good guys, you know? Those crooks who say, 'No hard feelings for ruining my family and sending me to jail for the rest of my life.' Those I trust not to send a hit man after me. With those I correspond weekly. Tell them all about my great life spent watching the mountains in Wyoming not move."

"So what's so bad about semiretiring to the beautiful state of Wyoming? You're seventy-two."

"Seventy-four. Thanks to you. If I never met you, I'd still be forty-seven, probably."

"Not likely. Jake Burger tells me you're training two new contenders."

"Beef cattle. Two-legged beef cattle. That's all they have out here: beef cattle. Four-legged beef cattle, two-legged beef cattle."

"If you don't have hope for them, you wouldn't be training them."

"Beef cattle marked U.S.D.A. In this case, U.S.D.A. means You Should see how Dumb they Are."

"Maybe they'll win at the county fair."

"Not even in their weight class."

"How old are they? Twenty?"

"Sixteen. Eighteen. I won't live long enough to see either of them snooze on the canvas for the count of ten."

"I'll bet they're good."

"The older one, the eighteen year old, Haja, he calls himself, thinks gettin' mad at himself is the point of the game. He'd knock himself out, if I ever showed him how. The other one, the sixteen year old, Ricky, actually thinks his muscles are pretty, if you'd believe it."

"Doesn't every sixteen year old?"

"The only opponent that interests him is in the mirror. And he likes him too much to get close. Even though they're both wearing deodorant. Can you believe that? Ever hear of a boxer who insists on wearing underarm in the ring?"

"Sounds like a good idea to me."

"I keep saying, 'Why do I smell petunias in here? Phew!'"

"Sparring, which one usually wins?"

"Neither of 'em. The young one keeps dancin' like a city boy barefoot on a hot pavement so his pretty face won't get hit. The other one keeps gettin' so mad at himself for not connecting with the younger one that he bursts his own blood vessels. I tell you no lie."

"I'd like to drive out to look at them."

"No, sir! Don't waste my time."

"And bring a lady with me."

"Don't waste your time driving out here, from wherever you are. Even if you're at my front gate. I won't have you."

"She's a heavyweight."

"No, sir! Not at my camp!"

"She needs training."

"No, sir. I'm not ready for that. I never will be! Not in my camp! I've seen those magazines. Uh, uh."

"We'll see you in a few days."

"You will not. You show up here, Fletch, and I'll sic my two fighters on you, both Haja and Ricky, at the same time."

"That's no threat."

"You'd better believe it is."

"Naw," Fletch said. "You've already told me their flaws."

Fletch remained in the van's driver's seat.

The two attendants he had tipped rolled Crystal Faoni in an oversized wheelchair onto the hydraulic lift on the side of the van. He listened to the sound of the lift raising Crystal. The van tipped with her weight. In the back of the van they helped Crystal onto the large bed. The head of the bed was behind

Fletch's seat. They rolled the wheelchair back onto the lift and Fletch lowered it, and them, then raised the lift again and folded it within the van. They slid the van's side door closed.

One of the attendants looked through the van's open window. "Okay, buddy. Get her out of here."

Slowly, Fletch drove the van along the driveway of Blythe Spirit. There were still many vehicles in the driveway. Entering the road, he turned right toward the highway.

He heard Crystal sniffing. She blew her nose. Somewhere she must have found a box of tissues.

On the highway he accelerated.

Crystal asked, "Where are you taking me?"

"Wyoming."

There was a long pause. "Fletch? Is that you, Fletch?"

"You were expecting Charon maybe?"

"I thought you left."

"I said I wouldn't return to your room. Argue with you anymore."

"You always leave."

"Not if anyone really wants me. You didn't really want me to leave, did you?"

"No." She laughed. "What's in Wyoming?"

"Not much, according to Mister Mortimer."

"Who's Mister Mortimer?"

"A cranky old man named Mortimer who has always insisted everybody call him 'Mister.'"

"A friend of yours?"

"Yeah. He hates me. He's sure to hate you, too."

"Then why are we going there?"

"Best idea I've got. He probably doesn't realize it, but he's been adjusting people's weight all his life. He's a trainer. For boxers."

"A boxing coach?"

"Yeah."

"You're taking me to a training camp for boxers?"

"Yeah. I thought we'd try it. If that doesn't work, we'll try something else. You wouldn't mind developing your uppercut, would you?"

"What's an uppercut?"

"A slash over the eyebrow."

"I don't want any of those."

"The head of your bed raises and lowers."

"Oh, yeah."

He heard the electric motor raise the head of her bed.

"You can see out the windows. Nice scenery?"

"Yeah. The back of billboards."

"All the fronts say is KEEP AMERICA BEAU-TIFUL."

"Jeez," Crystal said. "He wants to turn me into a boxing champion."

"Hey, lady," Fletch said. "In your weight class, you're a shoo-in."

"Fletch? Can we stop so you can get me something to eat?"

"Sure," Fletch said. "I'm hungry, too."

"If I'm going to take up boxing," Crystal said, "I'll need to keep my strength up."

5

The woman in the black bikini who came to swim in the Olympic-sized outdoor pool kept glancing at Jack.

Dressed only in the white shorts with vertical blue side stripes he had been given and told to wear as a condition of his employment, Jack was cleaning the pool.

At each end of the pool as she swam laps, she managed to roll her eyes up for another look at him.

Jack had been told there were many conditions of his employment at Vindemia.

Arriving in that area of Georgia, he was surprised to learn that the village of Vindemia was on the estate of Vindemia itself, and one needed a pass to visit even the village. The three thousand, five hundred acre estate was entirely surrounded by chain link fence. There was only one entrance, and that was guarded.

Before he left Virginia, spending some of his earnings from Global Cable News, Jack bought some clothes, and, a used blue Miata convertible. On his way to Georgia he had stopped at Subs Rosa in North Carolina for Eat-in and Take-out.

The town nearest Vindemia was Ronckton. There he had lunch in a coffee shop. He asked if there were any jobs to be had in the area. The woman behind the counter said, "Only on the estate, really," and sent him to an accountant's office down the street.

"You should just fit the bill," the estate's accountant, Clarence Downes, said at first sight of Jack. He had just returned from lunch. "Come in and sit down. Let's talk."

In his office, sitting behind his desk, Downes' first question was, "Ever been in prison?"

"No, sir."

"We'll check on it."

"Sure."

"Any diseases?"

"I had chicken pox when I was a kid. I'm better now, thank you."

"Can you swim?" Smiling with approval, the heavy man had already surveyed Jack's body.

"Yes, sir."

"Sure you can. Play tennis?"

"Yes, sir."

"Any good?"

"I'm very big with the racquets."

Downes grinned. "What are you, takin' time off from college?"

"Trying to raise some money, sir."

"Sure. I've got two kids of my own in college. Good thing I'm a Certified Public Accountant. Damn-all, the bills never stop. I've never had to juggle my personal accounts before I had two kids in college at the same time. Where are your folks, John?"

"My mother has a medical problem, sir. My father has a small farm."

"I see. And you're not much on farm laboring, I expect. It's dry work, all right. I escaped a farm when I was a kid." The man slapped the side of his stomach. "I wanted to wear a white shirt and have a gut." He laughed. "See? I'm a success!"

"Yes, sir."

"Hmm." The man frowned a little at Jack's agreement. "So the job's on the Vindemia Estate. You know about it? Owned and closely operated by Doctor Chester Radliegh. So big it just about drives the whole economy around here. They need a young man—'presentable' is the description I was given—to keep the swimming pools, tennis courts, gymnasium clean, act as lifeguard when necessary, you know, if there are little kids around, be able to partner at tennis when someone who wants to play doesn't have a partner, help the gardeners out when necessary, help patrol the grounds when necessary—"

" 'Patrol the grounds'?"

"Yeah. Doctor Radliegh is a nut on security."

"You mean, with a gun and dog?"

"And walkie-talkie. Can you handle that?"

"I guess."

"And, when required, if there's a big party goin' on, or somethin', put on a white jacket and help serve drinks, whatever."

"Do I get paid extra for smiling?"

More slowly, Downes said, "And report to Doctor Radliegh's secretary anything you see that strikes you as out of the ordinary."

"What does that mean?"

"I tell you, Doctor Radliegh is a nut on security. He likes to know everything . . . about what everybody is doin', sayin'." He shrugged his shoulders. "He's just funny that way."

"Spy on the guests? Family?"

"There are conditions to your employment." Downes put on his glasses and referred to a list that seemed a permanent part of his desk top. "You will not be allowed to smoke, drink, or use other drugs, illegal substances, of course, or bring them onto the estate. Okay so far?"

"How about bubble gum?"

"The estate's colors are blue and white. We give you the clothes to wear and you wear them. You don't wear any other clothes while you're on the estate, even if and when off duty. Got that?"

"Okay, but no tutus."

"Old man Radliegh runs that estate like a nineteenth century British Man of War."

"What happened to the last guy who had this job?"

"Two empty beer cans were found in the waste-basket in his room."

"For that he was fired?"

"Instantly."

"Not hung from the yardarm?"

"You are not to bring personal guests onto the estate. You are not to bring a woman to your quarters. Even if you help a woman guest in the gym, or play tennis with her, you are not to develop a personal relationship with her."

"Phew. Why doesn't old Radliegh run the estate with robots?"

"I think he would if he could. You'll live in half of a divided cottage, your own room, bath and kitchenette. It is expected you will do all your food shopping at the estate general store in the village of Vindemia."

"I'm expected to sell my soul to the company store?"

"It's not a bad deal, really. The store on the estate is nonprofit. You buy retail at wholesale prices. Plus, Doctor Radliegh himself has checked the nutritional value of all the food sold, for example. It's the best."

"No junk food?"

"Potato chips. He likes potato chips himself. You may use the gymnasium, pool, etc., but not while a member of the family or guest is using them. Unless you have an explicit reason for being someplace, if a member of the family or a guest appears, you are to disappear. You have a car?"

"Yes."

"When you arrive, you will park it in the locked compound, and turn over your keys. Radliegh doesn't want unnecessary traffic on the estate. Bicycles are available. You'll have from midnight Wednesday until midnight Thursday off. If you choose to leave the estate during that time, of course your car will be made available to you."

"This is Thursday."

"So it is." Downes told Jack the rate of pay. He began to hand Jack a closely printed sheet of paper. "Is all this agreeable to you?"

"Where do I sign?"

After a little more paperwork with Clarence Downes, Jack drove to the estate.

The erections holding the wrought iron gates to the estate were thirty five meters high. Stucco walls ten meters high extended out of sight in each direction. The gatehouse itself was as big as a suburban executive mansion.

"Is this The Magic Kingdom?" Jack asked the blue-and-white uniformed guard.

"You almost got it right," the guard said. "You got a pass?"

"Yeah." Jack handed the guard his laminated pass. "Winnie the Pooh dropped his."

Jack's pass was pink, Downes had told him, to identify him as an employee.

At least a mile ahead of him, on a rise, the roofs

and other parts of the main house were visible. The roofs were blue tile. In the sunlight, the white walls of the house gleamed like an actor's teeth. Several huge blue-and-white flags, visible even from that distance, flew in the breeze above the roofs.

The guard gave him directions to the car compound. "Go directly there," he said. "I'm phoning ahead. They'll expect you within six minutes. Do not drive over thirty miles an hour."

"What do I do about the car's exhaust?"

The guard grinned. "Bag it."

Driving the smooth road, landscaped both sides, Jack remembered his conversation with Global Cable News' Assistant to the Chief Executive Officer, Alex Blair. Jack had said he was not married or otherwise entangled and was free to go abroad.

Entering Vindemia he felt as if he had entered a foreign country. Very foreign.

He had entered the sort of world God might have created if He had money, to use an old wheeze.

A car the likes of which Jack had never seen before passed him coming from the main house. It was a chauffeur driven extended Infiniti.

An older woman in a picture hat sat alone in the back seat. She held a handkerchief to her nose. Was she weeping?

The limousine oozed along silently at exactly thirty miles an hour.

"Woo," Jack said to himself. " 'Round here, I'd better not accept any apples from women, or I just might end up somewhere well east of here."

Having finished her laps in the pool, the girl in the black bikini swam to the pool edge near Jack. She folded her arms on the pool edge. She rested her chin on her forearms.

She had coal-black hair, very wide-set coal black eyes.

Standing on the edge of the pool, Jack was vacuuming the pool's bottom with a wide, long hose.

Already he was tired of hearing the huge flags over the main house cracking in the wind.

There was no one else in the pool area.

She said, "Hi."

"Hello, Miss."

"Let me see the back of your leg."

"Do I have to do that, too?"

"Turn around."

He turned around.

He knew she was looking for the small blue eye tattooed on the calf of his left leg just below the knee.

"I thought you look familiar."

"I am, Miss. Some people say, Much too."

After watching him another minute, she lifted herself out of the pool.

She said, "Fletch."

"Jack Faoni, Miss. Nice of you to remember me, Miss."

Her low, warm voice said, "Who'd ever forget?"

"I didn't," he said.

"We had fun that night."

"Yes, Miss."

"Great fun. I mean, it was really nice. Did you bring your guitar?"

"Yes, Miss."

"Do you work here?"

"Yes, Miss."

"When did you arrive?"

"Last night, Miss."

Standing a meter away from him on the pool edge, she looked up at part of the main house. "I thought you were going to be my cousin."

Jack lowered his voice's register. "It would never have worked. I would have had to meet with you, learn everything about your family, who I would be in that family . . ."

"You'd rather work here than be a guest here?"

"I'm freer this way. Anyway, who wants to be all that polite all the time? Occasionally, I'm given to flatulence."

"That would never do," she said.

Shana Staufel sat in a long chair two meters behind him. His back to her, he continued working.

They continued talking softly, conversationally.

"Nice of you to come," she said.

"What am I doing here?"

"As stated," Shana said. "Weird things are happening. The people here have everything anybody could possibly want, looks, brains, health, prestige, every toy in the world, and yet the tension is so thick I don't think you could cut it with a chain saw."

"Aren't the spoiled always discontented?"

"I'm talking about resentment, cruelty, hatred, Jack, all aimed at a specific person."

"Who?"

"Chester Radliegh."

"The captain of the ship."

"I'm afraid the tension is bubbling over into violence. Covert violence."

"How long have you been here?"

"Ten days. At first, I thought what I was hearing from everybody was just a general, loving, humorous ribbing of the old man. Whenever he was out of earshot, everyone would begin muttering. Then I realized there was no humor intended. These comments were not being made with love, but with hatred. To them, Chester can say nothing right, do nothing right. If he says it's Tuesday, everyone complains and says it's Monday, or Wednesday, when, in fact, it is Tuesday, if you understand me. It's all rather unfair."

"Who is 'everybody'?"

"His wife. His children. He has his home office here, over by the golf course, airport. His chief executives, such as his chief executive officer, Eric Beauville, seem to be the same way: very nice to Chester's face, hateful toward him as soon as he turns his back."

"So Doctor Radliegh is a genius. You don't expect people around a genius to understand him. Of course there are misunderstandings."

"I tell you, it's dangerous. You know how it is

when you're boiling eggs, or spaghetti, and there's too much water in the pot, too much heat, and the water bubbles up to the rim of the pot?"

"Yeah, I've burned spaghetti."

"If you don't turn down the heat, it spills over, scalds the stove, douses the flame, whatever. That's the way it is here. The pot is just beginning to bubble over."

"What do you mean by 'covert violence'? Got any specifics?"

"Yes."

He heard her take a deep breath. "You going to make me ask?"

"Every morning a few minutes after dawn Chester rides his huge stallion madly over the hills, jumping the fences. I guess he does it to rid himself of tensions. The morning of the day I called you, while he was riding out of the stable yard, his horse keeled over dead. They say it died of a heart attack."

"Horses die of heart attacks."

"A three-year-old horse? I think he was drugged."

"Any proof?"

"Chester refuses to have a blood test done on the horse. I think he doesn't want to know."

Jack felt Georgia's summer sun crisping his shoulders. "That's not much."

"Chester has a one-room cabin in the woods up in the hills. He calls it his 'think house.' Every afternoon he goes there at four o'clock, and spends an hour by himself, unwinding, I guess, listening to Haydn. Yesterday afternoon shortly after four o'clock the cabin blew up. It exploded into matchsticks. They say the heater must have exploded."

"The heater?" Sweating, Jack squinted up at the sun. "Why would the heater be on in this weather?"

"You tell me."

"Was someone working on it?"

"Got me."

"I take it Doctor Radliegh was not in the cabin when it blew."

"On his way there, the front axle of the Jeep he was driving broke."

"Hum. If the front axle on the Jeep had broken when he was coming down from the cabin, would he have gotten hurt?"

"Probably killed. The road is unpaved, twisting, right on the edge of the hill much of the way. It was muddy yesterday afternoon."

"You count that as three possible attempts on his life."

"There was a fourth, this morning. Every morning before dawn, Chester makes his own coffee in his dressing room. This morning, he found the coffeepot unplugged. The plug was wet. The natural place he would have held on to the wire to plug it in had been scraped bare."

"How do you know this?"

"He complained of not having his morning coffee."

"These are a lot of coincidences."

"Too many, wouldn't you say?"

"I notice you call him 'Chester.' "

"Yes."

"You're the daughter-in-law-to-be. Wouldn't Doctor Radliegh, Professor Radliegh be more appropriate?"

"I knew Chester before I met Chet."

"Oh?"

"I worked as translator, interpreter for his interests in Europe."

"You traveled with him?"

"With his retinue. Acting as his interpreter at social functions, I was told to call him Chester. He said calling him Doctor, Professor was offputting for his other guests."

"I see."

"I came here to Vindemia in the spring to back up his home team while he was negotiating around the clock with some German and Scandinavian industrialists, members of governments. It was then I met Chet."

"Love at first sight?"

"I saw you were making a name for yourself as an investigative reporter, so I thought I'd give you a call. I didn't know what else to do. I'm worried." She paused. "Sorry to take advantage of such a short acquaintance, however intense."

Jack said, "I don't see what I can do. I can't walk around in front of him checking his horse's pulse and plugging in his coffeepot for him."

"Don't investigative reporters investigate?"

"Now I'm sorry I didn't come here as a guest. I'm too far removed from him, the family."

"Too late now."

"Doctor Radliegh was a professor of physics. He must have studied the Laws of Probability. What does he think of all these coincidences?"

"I think he's in some kind of denial. Is that the right expression? I've been abroad since I graduated. He is growing quieter."

"He seems a man of most regular habits."

"He lives by the clock. He has his own schedule and keeps to it, minute by minute. It's a part of his perfect self-discipline."

"That's dangerous. Seeing you talk to him, you might suggest he begin varying his schedule, become a little less predictable."

"That would be like asking a zebra to take off those silly looking pajamas."

"Or you might suggest he go away for a while, leave Vindemia altogether."

"His home is here. His laboratory. His home office. All his toys. Getting him to leave here is like taking a chocolate chip out of a cookie."

"He must know something is wrong. He's got to do something about it. He needs someone more than me."

"He is very protective of his family."

"I see that."

"I don't think he would accuse them of anything, have them suspected by anybody."

"But you, being the outsider, are alarmed."

Shana said, "Obviously, I'm just here to let the family get to know me, let me know them, test life here at Vindemia—"

"Do you like it here?"

"Who wouldn't?" She paused at length. "My own family is a mess. My father has been married four times, my mother, three. He's a lawyer in Albany. He gets away with anything he wants, drunken driving, fiddling documents, putting bought and paid for people on a jury. My mother has taken to sitting on a couch and eating a handkerchief a day. My sister is scarfing up all the drugs in South America, however she can get them. My brother is in prison. For rape. There's never been any discipline in my family at all. Except for me. I'm the rebel, I guess."

"And you admire discipline."

"Oh, yes."

"And you admire Doctor Radliegh."

"Who wouldn't? He's everything a man should be."

"And you love Chet?"

"Just by watching, listening, can't you figure out who is doing these things, why, put a stop to it?"

"I doubt it. Everyone here knows this place better than I. Everyone knows him, and his disciplined routine better than I." Jack looked up at what he could see of the huge house. "This place is a lot bigger than I ever could have imagined. I heard it was big, but this is ridiculous. I have an appoint-

ment with Doctor Radliegh's secretary in a few
minutes, and I don't even know how to begin to
find her. There doesn't even seem to be anyone
around to ask."

"She's over in the office building, by the airport.
Take a bike."

"Is there a map?"

"They didn't give you one?"

"I think they don't want me exploring."

"Will you try?"

"I'll watch," Jack said. "I'll listen. I'll think."

A man in his mid-twenties dressed only in tank
trunks entered the pool area. He was heavily muscled. He waved at Shana.

Jack said, "I doubt I'll accomplish anything."

The young man climbed to the highest diving
platform. Without hesitation, he dove, did a double
back flip and entered the water hardly rippling the
surface.

"Is that Chet?" Jack asked.

"Yes. Class valedictorian and All-American quarterback."

"Not what I was expecting."

"The National Football League made him an offer to play. He could buy his own team, of course.
Oxford offered him a full fellowship."

"Can he buy Oxford?"

"If his Daddy cosigned the note."

In one smooth movement as if continuing his
swimming stroke, Chet popped out of the pool and
landed on his feet on the deck. Dripping, he stood

on the pool deck arms akimbo. He said to Shana, "Time to go."

He did not appear to realize she and Jack had been talking to each other.

"Where?" she asked.

"You've had enough sun."

"Just resting after doing my laps. I've only been here a few minutes."

Although Chet put his hand out to Shana, he was looking at Jack.

Slowly he looked Jack up and down as if wondering how much he cost.

"All right." Lazily, Shana got up from the long chair.

When they left the pool area, Shana and Chet were walking a meter apart. He was chattering about some dance step. Twirling on the flagstone, he showed her how it was done.

At the gate, Chet looked back at Jack.

Frowning, Jack continued vacuuming the pool. The way Chet had looked at him made Jack uneasy.

6

Instead of answering the phone in the front seat of the van with a simple "hello" when it buzzed, Fletch sang to it, " 'Hello, America, how's by you . . . ?' "

"Mister Fletcher? This is Andy Cyst."

"How're you doin', Andy?"

"I'm fine, Mister Fletcher. How're you doin'?"

"Just gettin' by," Fletch sang, "Dancin' side by side . . ."

"You sound pretty relaxed, Mister Fletcher."

"Is modern man ever more relaxed than when whizzing along a highway at the speed of a hurricane?"

"I'm afraid not, Mister Fletcher."

"Terrifying, isn't it?"

"I never heard you sing before, Mister Fletcher."

"Now you know what you've missed."

"I have the information you requested on Ches-

ter Radliegh. Aren't you in the northwest somewhere?"

"Headed for Wyoming, Andy. Shall I sing 'Git
Along Little Dogies'?"

"If you want to."

"Maybe later."

"Chester Radliegh lives in Georgia."

"Ah, the state that originally banned lawyers.
And slavery. First came the lawyers. Then slavery.
Things haven't changed much since."

"On an estate called Vindemia. Very large, I
gather. It has its own golf course, employees' village—it's near a town called Ronckton. Are you on
vacation or something, Mister Fletcher?"

"From what?"

"I mean, you're nowhere near Georgia."

"Just transporting a friend who once transported
me." Fletch heard Crystal laugh on her bed in the
back of the handicap van. Through the dashboard
speaker she could hear the whole conversation.

"Okay." Andy took a big breath and began reading. "Chester Radliegh, aged fifty eight, second son
of Randolph and Melissa Radliegh, born in Lin-
coln, Massachusetts, to a well-off, established
American family."

"What does 'established' mean? Aren't we all 'established,' one way or another?"

"Establishment. His family showed the *May-
flower* where to anchor, or something."

"Ah! Native Americans!"

"His family always had been in either the ministry or banking."

"There's a difference?"

"Although he was a professor at Massachusetts Institute of Technology, his undergraduate, Master's and Ph.D. in physics were from Harvard. Incidentally, as an undergraduate at Harvard he was a two-letter man, fencing and baseball. He taught at Harvard, then at Jesus College at Oxford before teaching at MIT."

"So he's a literate, athletic scientist."

"A Renaissance man. Harvard. You know, he knows something about everything and everything about something."

"And nothin' about nothin' much."

"He invented the perfect mirror. How did he do that?" Andy asked.

"Somehow, he must have turned two negatives into a positive."

"What?"

"I don't know."

"The old-fashioned mirrors look weird now, don't they?"

"They were standard for centuries."

"Now they make your eyes cross."

"We never know what we're missing until someone sells it to us. Isn't that the truth?"

"Anyway, he had enough private funds to patent the perfect mirror himself, manufacture and market it himself. Which is why he's so rich."

"How rich?"

"Billions."

"Pretty rich."

"He has factories and other business interests all over the world. He built this huge estate in Georgia where he keeps his family, his home office, laboratory, and spends most of his time. He's known as a sort of restless art collector. He buys the world's best works of art, then is apt to tire of them and sell them. I guess he analyzes them, absorbs them, or something, then feels he doesn't need them anymore. At Vindemia he also is trying to develop a new breed of cattle, and, mule."

"Mule?"

"Mule. He married Amalie Houston when he was twenty-six, she twenty-three."

"Was she also academic?"

"She was a clerk at his father's bank in Boston. Academic? No. A few years ago, when she was on the board of directors of a juvenile detention center, she made a speech recommending that all boys up to age eighteen who had been found guilty of violent acts be neutered."

"Sexually neutered?"

"Castrated."

"Why only those up to age eighteen?"

"Juvenile detention centers only keep boys until they're eighteen. I guess she didn't want to appear overreaching."

"She'd spent too long amongst those mules. How about girls?"

"She stated that girls' violence was necessary to protect themselves."

"From boys who hadn't been castrated yet."

"Mrs. Radliegh claimed to have been misquoted."

"Was she?"

"No. Since then, she's held no public positions. Apparently, Radliegh is extremely conscious of his public image."

"Too bad. Given a free hand, she could have accelerated the emasculation of the American male considerably."

"It is not generally known, has never been published, but I understand she has been treated several times for acute depression, including electric shock therapy."

"Oh."

"It may just be a rumor, but I don't think so. She is considered eccentric, but she appears at public functions always hanging on to her husband's arm and smiling. She is known for saying wrong things. On a visit to the White House she is reported to have said to the President's wife, 'Really, my dear, you ought be paid for all that you do, or take to your bed.' "

"Was she invited back?"

"Of course. She's Chester Radliegh's wife. They have four children. The eldest, the daughter Amy, twenty-nine, has been married three times, and has seven children."

"Doesn't sound like she's much in favor of castration for anybody, does it? Does she live on the estate?"

"Yes, with all her kids. She's not presently married. Next in line is Chester Junior, football All-American and Phi Beta Kappa."

"Number 41," Fletch said. "Chet Radliegh. I never connected him with the perfect mirror."

"He is engaged to marry a girl named Shana Staufel. Bryn Mawr graduate who used to work for Radliegh Mirror in Europe as an interpreter. It is believed the old man is grooming young Chester for a congressional seat from their district in Georgia. A book has been written discussing the conflicts between the First and Fourteenth Amendments to the United States Constitution, a book which is to be published under young Chester's name."

"Has he been to Law School?"

"Yes, but he flunked his first attempt to pass the bar exam."

"So the book will be published as soon as he passes the bar?"

"It is whispered in the halls of Congress that the present incumbent of that particular congressional seat in Georgia has been offered an awful lot of money to retire. The source of this money is unknown."

"Smoke and mirrors," Fletch said.

"Young Chester is twenty-five. Next in line is daughter Alixis, aged twenty-three. After flunking out of Ol' Miss, where she was a cheerleader, Allied films produced a musical called *Feint at Heart* as a starring vehicle for her. Ever heard of it?"

"No."

"It didn't do well. It cost thirty-two million to produce and had a limited release one weekend last April. The kindest thing written about it was that it was 'old fashioned.' One reviewer wrote of her, I have it here, 'This is the ultimate, we hope, movie about the girl-next-door who should have stayed there—next door.' "

"Nasty, nasty. Some of these reviewers will say anything to be quoted."

"And then there's Duncan, aged twenty-one. He just graduated from Vanderbilt University at the bottom of his class. He likes racing cars, playing at being a mechanic. It is said he is to be a candidate for a Master's degree in Business Administration next fall, but no one seems to know where."

"The old man wants him to be able to take over and run the shop."

"On the other hand, he's paid his entrance fee to several car races throughout next year. He races something called 'The Mirror Car,' of which several versions have been made."

"Has he ever won a race?"

"Yes. One. In Utah. A five thousand dollar purse."

"That should pay expenses."

"At least for the nitrogas."

"It sounds as if they're all having fun."

"Does it?"

"Spending money anyway."

"Mister Fletcher, is there a story here, on Radliegh, his family, something?"

"You're wondering why I asked you to do this research, Andy."

"I mean, you're nowhere near Georgia."

"Keep your research on tap. One never knows."

"By the way, Mister Fletcher, that kid who worked with you on that story about the Tribe? Jack Faoni?"

"What about him?"

"He left here a couple of days ago."

"Where do you suppose he went?"

"He said he was going to North Carolina for lunch."

Smiling, Fletch asked, "What's so perplexing about that? Everyone gets hungry."

"He didn't even have a car."

"Well, Andy," Fletch said. "Some lunches are worth going out of your way for. Thanks for your work, my good man. I'll practice 'Git Along Little Dogies' so I can sing it for you next time. In the key of Lee Marvin."

He switched off the phone.

On her bed in the back of the van, Crystal asked, "Isn't Vindemia where you said Jack was going?"

"Yeah."

"What's he doing there?"

"Visiting the girl young Chester Radliegh intends to marry, I guess."

"Sounds risky."

"He has his guitar," Fletch said. " 'Music soothes the savage beast.' "

"Radliegh," Crystal said after the van had gone another ten miles. "First he creates the perfect mirror, then he tries to create the perfect image. The first was scientifically possible—"

"And the second," Fletch said, "is a goose's chase."

7

"**I**'m as old as water, and just as weak."

The very old woman in the sunbonnet had only glanced up at Jack as he came along the shady side of the swimming pool. She was on her knees on the lawn removing the very few weeds from the azalea border. She dug into the soil with bare fingers. She had no gardening tools. At first he thought she was talking to the plants.

"Plants; weeds," she continued muttering at the soil: "Just like children." She pinched a dead leaf off an azalea. "Nurture some plants beautifully, give them everything they want and need, and some of them just curl up ugly. Beat some weeds to death and they just keep popping up, growing, proliferating. If we had genuine respect for character, we'd cultivate weeds and send the plants to mulch." She sat back on her heels and looked up at where Jack stood, looking down at her. "Hello."

"Hello, Ma'am."

"Are you a weed, or a plant?"

Jack said, "I think I'm a weed."

"That's good. You look strong and resilient enough to be a weed, that you do. You're new here. I'm Mrs. Houston."

"Sorry, Ma'am. I don't recognize your name."

"Mother of Amalie Radliegh, Mrs. Radliegh. Grandmother to most of the big brats around here, great-grandmother to most of the little brats. I call the little brats, Amy's brats, 'The Sudden Seven.' I looked away for a moment and there they were."

"Maybe they're weeds," Jack offered.

"That would be nice. But I doubt it. Here at Vindemia she has them each bedded in rich nutrients and waters them daily, here at the pool. Weeds don't need as much as they have."

"Weeds can stand some good treatment, too," Jack said.

"I'm not so sure."

"I've had some," he said. "I'm still a weed."

"Looks like you've had some good nutrients, anyway." The old lady's blue eyes were looking at Jack as if she would know him in a minute. "What's your name?"

"Jack."

"Are you quick and nimble?"

"For a weed."

"Yes. I believe you are. Now I'm not supposed to be messing up the garden this way, I know that. Do you mind?"

"Not at all."

"But one has to do something. One can't just sit around all day and night being waited on hand and foot. At least I can't. One loses touch with oneself if one doesn't do work of some kind, some time. Don't you agree?"

"I suppose I would."

"I don't even want to go to heaven," Mrs. Houston said as she dug her fingers into the soil, "unless they have some work for me to do there."

"Is Vindemia pretty close to heaven?" Jack asked.

"All these people here dragging themselves from swimming pool to tennis court to gymnasium to the stables worrying about their figures, their skin tone, the shine of their hair. Do you know they don't even saddle their own horses?"

"I didn't know that."

"And do you think they're happy? Not a bit of it. Not one of them. You never heard such a chorus of complaining, weeping. I say to them, 'Make your own bed, get your own breakfast, saddle your own horse, clean your own car, go start a garden of your own: you'll feel better.' What do they complain about? That they're not allowed to be themselves." Mrs. Houston raised a soil-encrusted index finger to Jack. "I suspect they don't know who themselves are. Everything Chester asks them to do, expects them to do, they think is unfair. They think doing their duty is unfair! You know what my daughter says?"

"I've never met the lady."

"She asks, 'Why do I have to talk to the cook once a week? Why do I ever have to talk to the housekeeper? Why do I have to be at Chester's elbow every time he entertains all those boring people?' Can you believe that? I say, 'Because it's your job, daughter.' She says, 'But sometimes I don't feel like being nice to people. It can be inconvenient.' I tried to tell her that everything in life costs. Being Chester Radliegh's wife, living here, costs. She's got to pay the price, whatever it is, just like everybody else on this earth. She's got to do her duty. Extending herself to people important to him is little enough to pay for all she has."

"I'm glad to meet you, Mrs. Houston," Jack said. "I'm expected at Doctor Radliegh's secretary's office in a few minutes."

"You don't know the cost of things until you've had to work for everything you've ever had, as I did. When my husband died from overwork and hopelessness, I worked as a hotel maid from six in the morning until three, and after that in the hotel laundry to raise Amalie, send her through secretarial school. That was my duty, and I did it. My grandchildren just think all this is natural." Mrs. Houston's wave of her arm took in all Vindemia. "It just fell from the sky, as free as the sunlight and rain. They complain about their father, what he expects of them. I say, 'What if you were born in the slums? What if you were hungry every day? Would you complain as much then?' They say, 'It didn't happen.' "

The clock in the peak of the pool cabana's roof read twenty two minutes past twelve. He was due at the secretary's office at twelve thirty and he still didn't know where it was.

"Let me tell you," Mrs. Houston said to Jack, or the azaleas. "Chester is a sainted man. Out of his own genius and hard work he has created all this, given them everything they could want, and how do they thank him? They never have a smile for him, a kind word, not a lick of appreciation or respect. I'd like to see one of them do ten percent of what he's done. No, they think he's some kind of a hard taskmaster just because he expects them to behave decently and do their duty. I tell you."

"Doctor Radliegh must expect a lot from himself," Jack said.

"He does indeed."

"Maybe too much from them?"

"He expects something from them."

"I must go," Jack said. "I don't want to be fired on my first day of work."

Mrs. Houston said, "Here I am, hiding behind a hedge, digging around in a garden that doesn't need digging. The garden doesn't need digging, but I need the work of digging. I'll be damned if I let myself become a petunia like the rest of them. You won't tell on me?"

"Never," Jack said.

"Thing is," Mrs. Houston said to Jack, "I appreciate. I respect. I appreciate and respect Chester. I also respect myself."

"I see that," Jack said. "Thanks for your help."

• • •

On a bicycle assigned to him the night before when his car was locked in the compound, Jack coasted down a shaded slope to a wide and deep, well land-scaped building he supposed housed the business offices. He had spotted what appeared to be the top of a transmitter tower over the trees and went to find its base.

Beyond the big building was an airstrip with one big hangar next to a short control tower.

Around the big, landscaped building was a driveway wide enough for cars to park on it, neatly, without giving the appearance of a parking lot. There weren't that many cars anyway. There were more bicycles in bike stands than there were cars.

He rode his bike to the front of the building, noticing there was no sign identifying the building. He slipped the front wheel of his bike into a stand. As all the bikes were alike, he noted that his was in the thirteenth slot from the left.

"Hey, Jack!"

One of the two men coming out of the front door of the building was the man who had hired Jack the day before.

" 'Morning, Mister Downes."

Jack's folded t-shirt hung out of the waistband at the back of his shorts.

"Come meet Eric Beauville, Jack. This is the man who runs the world, as far as you're con-

cerned. Chief Executive Officer of most things
named Radliegh."

Shaking hands with Jack, Beauville did not smile.
"I don't run the world. I follow orders like everybody else. There's a computer list of new orders
on my desk at six o'clock every morning."

"Well." Downes hitched up his trouser waist.
"Working for Doctor Radliegh never leaves the
slightest doubt as to what is expected of one."

"At six a.m., six thirty a.m., eight a.m., eleven
a.m.," Beauville said, "two p.m., four p.m., eight
p.m., eleven p.m."

Downes laughed. "Yes. Well."

"Saturdays and Sundays included," Beauville
concluded.

"You here to see Ms. Dunbar?" Downes asked
Jack.

"I'm afraid I'm late. I—"

"No excuses accepted," Beauville said. "When
Chester built the lake over there he said henceforth
all excuses were to be deep-sixed in there. He said
he built it deep enough for every excuse we could
think up. He didn't want to hear them anymore."

"You're sweating," Downes said. "Why don't
you walk around the back of the building, try to
stay out of the air conditioning. Chester's office is
in the center. Ms. Dunbar will see you through the
window."

"She probably has your pink slip ready," Beauville said, "to fire you, if you're more than two
minutes late."

"I'm more than two minutes late," Jack said.

"Then nice having met you. Okay, Downes." Beauville headed for a gray BMW coupe. "Better go back to town after lunch and find us another whatever-he-is. Pool ornament?"

"Lunch first." Downes followed Beauville to the car.

"Yeah." Beauville opened the car door. "You don't want to miss lunch with Chester. Three sliced half pears, a glob of cottage cheese and iced tea."

Downes said, "I'll have a cheeseburger in town later." He appeared to be talking to himself. "Ketchup and onions."

"You're late."

Jack had walked halfway along the back of the building. The windows were tinted so he could not see the rooms inside.

All he could see in the windows was himself.

A sliding glass door had opened.

"Sorry," Jack said. "Want an excuse?"

"Not really." Nancy Dunbar, although trim enough in figure, had an unattractive face. Her forehead was low, her chin receded, her eyes were small and close together, her nose wide. Her face looked pinched at birth. "Do you have one?"

"I couldn't find anyone to give me directions. Do you have a map?"

"Yes." She reached inside the building. "You didn't start in time. Don't come in. The air conditioning will chill you. You're sweating. Don't bother putting on your shirt." Outside the building, she slid the glass door shut. She had a loose piece of paper in her hand. A purse dangled from her arm. "We'll go over there."

She handed Jack the map. He folded it and put it in his back pocket.

He went with her along a walk toward what he thought was another building. They went through an arch in the wall.

He found himself in a walled Japanese garden. Ordinary rocks surrounded by raked sand were spaced throughout it. Stone benches were placed along the meandering natural stone walk that went around and through it. Graceful trees with few leaves stood against the walls of the garden.

"Hey," Jack said. "This is nice."

"Are you artistic?" Nancy sat on the stone bench closest to the wall nearest the office building. "Raking this daily will be your chore." Quickly, she took a cigarette out of her purse and lit it. She inhaled deeply. "Try to vary the designs the rake makes in the sand, will you? If you rake it the same way every day, Doctor Radliegh will notice and mention to me that you are a bore with a rake."

"I guess that's better than being a rake with a bore."

She glanced at him. She said: "Humor."

"I'm not fired?"

"For being late?" She exhaled a large amount of smoke. "Not this time."

"I didn't think so," Jack said. "You're smoking."

"Right," she said. "Not permitted. Care for a cigarette?"

"No, thanks."

She was putting the ash from her cigarette into a Ziploc bag she had taken from her purse.

"Now, then, I assume Downes gave you all the do's and don'ts regarding working here."

"Mostly don'ts," Jack said.

"This garden is your chore, the outdoor pool, the indoor pool, gymnasium, saunas, whirlpool, tennis courts. You're expected to help out the gardeners when they ask, also the indoor help, in the event of too many guests, or a party. There will be a party here Saturday night. You don't mind putting on a white jacket and handing around canapes, do you?"

"I'll have to sample them first," Jack said, "so I'll feel good about sharing them with the guests."

"Who has talked to you here so far?"

"Mrs. Houston."

Nancy smiled. "She's about the only reasonable one here. She's my good friend. What did she say to you?"

"She may have been talking to the azaleas."

"Ah!" Nancy smiled again. "She really opened up on you."

"Or the azaleas."

"You can forget whatever she says."

"Okay."

"Her loyalty is unquestioned. Who else has spoken to you?"

"A young woman who swam in the pool this morning. And a young man joined her. He didn't speak to me. Is she called Shana?"

"And Chet. Chester Junior. What did Shana say to you?"

"She asked if I worked here, when did I arrive, that sort of thing."

"They are affianced."

"Going to marry up with each other," he said.

"Yes. Exactly that. Anyone else?"

"No. I found my quarters last night. Ate my sandwiches. Walked around. I saw no one at all, except the guard at the gate who let me in."

"You won't be that lonely," she said. "Didn't you find the staff recreation hall?"

"No."

"Ping-Pong. Stereo. Billiards. Wide-screen t.v. Quite nice, really."

"Oh, wow."

"The thing is that you are not wanted around when members of the family or guests are present, unless there is a need for you. On the other hand . . ." She put out her cigarette against the sole of her shoe. No ashes fell to the ground. She must have practiced this maneuver. She put the filter into her little plastic baggy. Immediately, she lit another cigarette. ". . . if you notice anybody acting oddly, saying anything odd, you are to come and tell me."

"You mean, if I see someone breaking the rules?"

"Yes. That, of course. But I'm speaking of members of the family and guests as well as staff."

"Like Mrs. Houston?"

"Not Mrs. Houston. She is the exception. But that sort of thing, yes. We want to know of any plans you hear anybody make. If you see people together you think don't belong together, we want to know. We want to know of comments you hear people make about each other, Mr. Beauville, me, Doctor Radliegh. That sort of thing."

"Why?"

"Doctor Radliegh does not like surprises."

"That's the simple answer?"

"Yes."

"What about people's privacy?"

"Oh, all this information is private. If I think it necessary, I will pass it on to Doctor Radliegh, but it goes no farther than him."

Jack did not say anything. Granted, odd things were going on, possibly four attempts on Radliegh's life. He did not want Nancy Dunbar to know he had been told of them. Perhaps some such precautions were necessary.

The idea of his spying was hateful to him.

Yet that was why he was there, wasn't it?

"Is all this clear?" Nancy asked.

"Yes."

There was the sound of a siren.

Nancy's eyes widened. "Oh, my God."

Quickly, she ground the cigarette out against her shoe, dumped the bent filtered cigarette in her baggy, dropped that in her purse, snapped her purse shut, stood up and began running toward her office.

Jack walked rapidly after her.

After the sunlight in the garden, her office was cold and dark. It took him a moment to see in the room.

She stood at her desk, talking on the telephone. "Yes ... Yes ... And Doctor Radliegh was not there? ... I see ... Thank you," she said. "I'll take care of it."

After she hung up, Jack said, "What?"

"Doctor Jim Wilson was overcome by some sort of gas in the laboratory. The ambulance has come for him."

The phone rang.

"Yes?" she said into the receiver. "Yes ... ? I see. I'll take care of it."

Slowly, she hung up.

To Jack, or to herself, she said, "Jim Wilson is dead."

Jack said nothing.

"Odd," Nancy Dunbar said.

"Yes," Jack said. "What do you say is odd?"

"Doctor Radliegh always arrives first in the laboratory. He wants the time alone before Jim comes in at two o'clock." She looked at her watch. "It's only one-thirty. Normally, Doctor Radliegh would be there alone."

Jack said, "That's five."

• • •

Standing on the road on one leg, his other leg draped over his bike's boy bar, Jack watched people assemble in front of the hacienda-style laboratory across the road from Radliegh's main offices.

Back doors open, the ambulance was parked in front of the building.

Jack assumed the ambulance attendants had entered the building to recover the body of Doctor Jim Wilson. Some of the building's windows had been smashed, presumably to let the lethal gas escape.

Down the road at high speed rode a man on a bicycle. In his late fifties, he was tall, slim, broad-shouldered. His hair was salt and pepper gray and black. He wore horn-rimmed glasses.

Jack saw a tongue of flame spurt from a broken window on the first floor of the building.

"Hey!" Jack pointed at the window, at the flame.

The older man dropped his bike on the lawn and ran toward the building's front door.

"Hey!" No one was paying attention to Jack.

Smoke was now rushing through that window.

The older man collided with the ambulance attendants rushing out of the building at the front door.

The older man tried to push past them.

One attendant tried to grab his arm.

"No, Doctor Radliegh!" the attendant yelled. "Fire!"

Radliegh pushed the attendant away. "Jim Wilson! Is he dead?"

The other attendant fell to his knees on the lawn, coughing.

"Smoke!" the attendant yelled. "The building's on fire! Stay out of there!"

Radliegh disappeared into the building.

"Oh, my God, no," a woman on the sidewalk said. She screamed: "Doctor Radliegh! No!"

The attendant who had tried to stop Radliegh seemed pushed backward from the smoke rushing out of the open door.

For a moment, except for the soft wind noise of the flames and the smoke coming through the door and some of the smashed windows, there was silence.

Then there was an enormous bang. Just the sound made the people in the road jump back and duck their heads.

Tiles from the building's roof shot into the air.

The first story walls of the laboratory's main section blew out. The second story walls collapsed inward from their tops as if pulled by cables.

"No!" screamed the woman.

Pieces of the roof fell into the building, sending both smoke and dust into the sky.

"Doctor Radliegh!" The weeping woman turned her back to the building. She embraced another woman. "The boss . . ."

Jack looked at his watch.

It was one-fifty.

Smoke at one side of the building swirled like fog.

Through that smoke walked the older man.

In his arms he carried the limp body of another man.

The building's collapse almost had put out the fire.

Still, the air was thick with smoke and dust.

Walking heavily, smoke-stained, Radliegh carried the body of Doctor Jim Wilson to the ambulance.

Quietly, the people watched him.

Gently, Radliegh placed the body as well as he could on the floor of the back of the ambulance. Bent at the knees, the corpse's legs dangled over the road.

Radliegh turned. In a low voice, simply, he said to the people, "He is dead."

Slowly, he picked up his bicycle. Without glancing at the destroyed laboratory, he walked the bike across the street and neatly put it in the rack.

Then he entered the office building.

To himself, Jack said, "Six?"

8

"**Y**ou all right?" Jack asked.

"Allergies," the woman managed to say in a strangled voice. "You have to show me your I.D."

Jack took his laminated pink Vindemia identification out of his pocket and showed it to her.

"I guess I'd better look around." Jack put his shopping list in his pocket.

She handed him back his identification tag. "Help yourself."

Through the window of the Vindemia General Store Jack saw a white hearse park against the curb. Two men dressed in black slacks and white shirts were getting out of its front doors.

While riding the bike from the airport/office complex, silently a race car had drawn alongside Jack. It was going not much faster than Jack's bicycle. It oozed by him. Jack stood astraddle his bike on the road and looked after it. Almost every bit of the car, from hubcaps to windows, appeared to be mirrors. The sun reflecting from it stabbed his eyes painfully a half dozen times before it turned a corner and disappeared into an impeccably planted tree forest. He never heard the engine.

At the edge of the village, there was an intersection. The road to his left went one block, and, at a right angle, turned right. The road to his right went one block, and, at a right angle, turned left. The houses on both sides of the road, each in its own lot, were not identical, but very similar white cottages with blue roofs and trim, a bit of garden, a bit of lawn. Some of the cottages, like his own near the main house, appeared to be duplexes. None of the cottages had a driveway or garage. Crossing the road into the village, Jack figured these residences were built in a perfect square around the village's center.

The center of the village of Vindemia was only a block long. Landscaping made it look bigger. The buildings were placed precisely on their sites, in relation to each other, more as if a child had placed them for his toys rather than as if there had ever been any sort of human, evolutionary growth to the place, response to the location, the land itself.

The road was a smooth black; the sidewalks glaring white.

Besides the trimmed lawns, bushes, cultivated flowers, everything in the village, including the several fire hydrants, was glossy, eye-stabbing white in the sunlight, with blue roofs and trim.

There were metal bicycle racks everywhere.

"A pound of baloney, please."

"Oh, honey, we don't have baloney." The woman behind the counter of the Vindemia Village General Store coughed until her eyes ran. "Sliced ham. We have sliced ham."

"Isn't that a lot more expensive?"

She sneezed. "Of course." Her brown hair was thin on her scalp. The bags under her eyes complemented the general puffiness of her face. Her skin was gray. "Just healthy food," she coughed. "Health food."

"I like baloney." Jack looked at his short shopping list. "You have canned tuna fish? I like tuna puffs."

"No canned anything." She was choking.

There were no cars in the village.

At the end of the main street nearest the only gate to the estate (perhaps a mile away) was a fire station. Its doors were open. One large, one small fire truck had passed Jack on the road. They were headed for the laboratory, at thirty miles an hour. Next to the fire station was the General Store, with gasoline, diesel, and three air pumps, a phone booth, and three electric charging outlets neatly arranged outside. Beyond that was the church. It had a short steeple, a belfry, but otherwise was unadorned by any religious symbol, signboard, name. Next to it in its own bed of rhododendrons snuggled the library, low, with a low slanting roof and leaded windows. Then there was the school. Its windows were tinted glass. None were open. No

sound emanated from the school. The side yard of
the school nearest the library had picnic tables and
instructional areas under pine trees. The further
side of the school had seesaws, swings, and jungle
gyms. Behind the school was a football field surrounded by a cinder running track, and a baseball
diamond. The lawns appeared unscuffed.

Across the road from these buildings was a recreation area. Handball courts along the sidewalk
did not conceal an Olympic-sized swimming pool
behind them. Behind the swimming pool, behind
low hedges, were four tennis courts. There were
drinking fountains enough, Jack noticed, but no
soft drink machines. A large recreation hall was
placed sideways to the road. Overlooking these activity areas was the recreation building's wide, deep
veranda, dotted with blue rocking chairs. The recreation building itself, Jack could see from the road,
obviously had a large main room behind the veranda. On one end of the building, lower than the
main hall, was a locker, shower, changing room for
women; at the other end, one for men. Jack saw no
evidence of a snack bar or other food service. The
entrance to the recreation hall was on the other
side of the building, canopied, facing a small parking lot. At two o'clock on Friday afternoon, the
place was empty.

Across the parking lot from the recreation hall
was a small clinic. Next to it, the ambulance garage
doors were also open.

At the end of the road (it was a dead end) was a

tower, taller than anything else in the village. In the tower, facing the village, was a huge digital clock showing the hour, the minute, the second, and the millisecond. Even in the shaded bright sunlight the frantic whirring of the milliseconds dial provided the otherwise still village with an impression of activity.

Riding back to the General Store, Jack decided this would be called a designed community. Designed on a board in a brightly lit, air conditioned office, with pencil and ruler, or maybe on a computer screen. Designed with all the engineering essentials in place, not all of the human essentials, places for people to neck, fight, laugh, scream, cry, hide. There were birds in the trees, and a few tanned children idling about, but there were no dogs, cats, squirrels visible in the village. Except for the whipping of the big blue and white flag atop the clock tower, the place was as quiet as ice on a December pond.

As he pushed his shopping cart toward the produce section, he heard the two men from the hearse enter the store. "Hi, Marie."

"Frank." A sneeze. "Junior."

"How're the allergies doin'?"

"They're gettin' healthier." The woman behind the counter blew her nose. "They're gettin' healthier, and I'm gettin' sicker."

"Came out to pick up Doctor Wilson. Got gassed to death."

"I heard." Marie sniffled. "Didn't know there

was such a thing as lethal gas on this place."

"In the laboratory," one of the undertakers said. "In the lab."

"What was it?" Marie asked. "The gas, I mean."

"Damned if I know. Enough to set fire to the place. Blow it up."

"Was that the big noise I heard?"

"The lab. building blew up."

"I guess some thought ol' Radliegh was in the building when it blew," the other man from the hearse said. "He wasn't."

"Too bad," Marie said.

The store's fresh produce, Jack realized, clearly was untouched by any beautifying chemicals. Tangerines and oranges were spotted yellow and black; the tomatoes, even in that season, were more yellow and green than red; the bananas more green or black than yellow; the apples yellow and green, none shiny red. The carrots looked like carrots.

"You got Wilson in the hearse?" Marie asked.

"Yeah."

The shelves indeed stocked no canned foods, not even soups or boxes of cereal. There were bags of potato chips, tins of dry mustard, but no ketchup; olives, but no pickles; peanut butter but no marshmallow.

There was no candy counter.

"So what did you stop for?" Marie asked. "If we had chawin' tobacco or beer, which we surely don't, you know I couldn't sell it to you any which way."

The only toothpaste available had a baking soda

base. There were soaps available, but no sprays.

"I was wonderin' if I could buy some of your roast beef," one of the undertakers said.

"You know I can't sell it to you, Frank."

"I married your sister, Marie."

"Thank you, but I can only sell to employees and guests of the estate, Frank. You know that."

The jars of instant coffee were all decaffeinated except the acid free Kava. The teas were all herbal.

"I'm a relative of an employee, Marie," Frank said: "You."

"Doesn't count." Marie sneezed.

"Marie doesn't count," Junior said.

"Frank doesn't count," Marie said.

The only patent medicine available was Bayer's aspirin. There were shelves and shelves of generic vitamins and herbal goods, fresh, whole, dried cranberry juice concentrated extract tablets, lycopodium, echinacea, et cetera, round containers of protein powders. Printed lists along these shelves described the uses and benefits of each selection offered.

"Pretend you're buyin' it for yourself," Frank said.

Marie coughed. "Can't do that. These walls have ears."

White bread was not available in that store.

"Sure," Frank said. "We're allowed on the estate when a body needs pickin' up, a gassed body, but rules say I can't go home to a supper of the best beef for a hundred miles around here?"

"Rules say." Marie blew her nose. "Employees only."

The meat counter offered 91-percent-lean hamburger only, ground beefalo meat, especially lean-looking steaks, other cuts of beef, chops. All the chicken offered was in packets, and was skinless. The prices for these meats were lower than usual. The only fish was pond-bred catfish. There were no sausage, bacon, hot dogs or pressed meats available.

A telephone rang.

Marie said, "Hello? . . . Yes, he's here. I'll tell him." She said, "That was Nancy Dunbar."

"The bitch," Frank said.

" 'I'll take care of it,' " Junior mimicked in a falsetto. " 'I'll take care of every-thing.' "

He sounded more like a parrot than he did Nancy Dunbar.

So Jack collected his groceries: lettuce, carrots, celery, 100 percent Real Mayonnaise, a gallon of mixed vegetable juices, oranges, apples, bananas, pumpernickel, mustard, sliced ham, ground beefalo meat, a steak, a small packet of boneless, skinless chicken, 2 percent skim milk, butter, eggs, some cheese. He did not take a bag of potato chips.

"Marie," Frank said, "when you croak, who do you suppose is going to come along and carry off your moral demains?"

"Not you, I hope. You stop on your way back to the shop leavin' a corpse sweatin' in the back of your wagon."

"None other but me," Frank said.

"I'll outlive you by a hundred years."

"Not the way you cough and sneeze. You don't ever sound like you'll make it to next payday, Marie, I do declare. How do you go on?"

"I'm developin' life-savin' muscles," Marie said.

"For sure, you're the sickest thing I ever saw in a health store."

"Life-savin' respiratory muscles," Marie coughed.

The hardware section of the General Store had the simplest tools neatly arranged, none electrical.

Jack dropped a blue knapsack into his shopping cart.

Frank said, "Don't come to my house Sunday for spaghetti."

Marie said, "It's my sister who invites me. Not you."

The men returned to the hearse.

The magazines arrayed were as genuine as news magazines get, some science fiction but no tabloids, purely gossip, romance, horoscopes or other kinds of comic books. The paperbound books offered were all classics. Even the mysteries were classics.

Marie said to Jack, "You're funny, or somethin', aren't you?"

"Sure," Jack answered.

She was adding up his bill. "John Funny, or somethin'?"

"Jack Faoni."

"Yeah." Marie sneezed. She wiped her nose with

the back of her hand, which held his beefalo burger. "Ms. Dunbar called for you. You're to report to the tennis courts up by the main house. Ms. Alixis wants to play with you."

"Oh, wow," Jack said. "Who's Ms. Alixis?"

"Our movie star. You want to play with a movie star?" She grinned.

"I have a choice?"

"Second daughter," Marie said. "Alixis Radliegh. She was in a movie. *Feint at Heart*, spelt funny, the French way, or something. In it she wandered around in shorty pajamas singing to something or other in the trees until this hunk named Heathcliff fell out of a tree, nearly beaned her, but he had a broken neck or something so she had to nurse him back to health, if you know what I mean, by singing to him in her cabin by the lake. So they could make beautiful music together. I saw it. It stank."

"I must have missed that one."

"It stank. It was shown here on the estate. Terrible movie. But we told her how proud we are of her."

"This is one of Doctor Radliegh's daughters? A movie star?" Jack was fitting his groceries into his knapsack.

Marie sneezed. "You think my sneezin' will get me anything if I do enough of it in shorty pajamas under a tree?"

"Maybe," Jack said. "Maybe you'll be beaned by a hungry undertaker."

Marie said, "I knew you were listening."

Outside, fitting his new knapsack onto his back, climbing on his bike, Jack noticed a candy bar wrapper next to the curb.

9

The short tanned girl with short dark hair wearing a short white tennis skirt watched Jack approach without apparently blinking in the full sunlight. She stood by a net on one of the tennis courts. Three racquets leaned against the net. At her feet was a bag of balls.

She had just stood by the net, waiting, not practicing her serve or using the backboard. She didn't even have a racquet in hand.

"Shana told me about you," she said. "At lunch."

"I'm Jack."

"I know."

He picked up one of the three racquets. "Are we expecting someone? Playing Canadian doubles?"

"No. I just thought I'd give you a choice of racquets."

"Thanks."

Coming out of the General Store in the village of Vindemia, Jack had noticed a uniformed security guard using the public pay phone.

Before going to the tennis courts Jack had bicycled his groceries back to his quarters, stored them in the small refrigerator, small cupboards. He ate a ham sandwich with a glass of milk.

"Let's just rally, shall we?" he asked.

"Okay." Alixis' voice was bored, indifferent.

Watching her across the net playing tennis, Jack saw that Alixis had been beautifully taught. Her legs were excellent, muscular, springy.

But either she was awfully tired or awfully lazy. Unless his shot bounced within a convenient few steps of her, she ignored it.

After a few minutes, he asked, "Shall we play a game?"

"No," she answered. "Let's just sit. I'm hot."

"Okay."

She sat on a bench in the sunlight at the side of the court.

She said, "This will permit me to tell my father I spent time on the tennis court this afternoon."

"Is that required?"

"Required?" A light breeze blew against her short hair. "You mean, do we have to sign in, punch a clock? Not exactly. But it is well to mention casually our day's activities in front of my father: time spent swimming, in the gym, on the tennis courts, in the library."

"Why?"

"If we don't, if he doesn't think we are obeying his philosophy of daily living, balancing physical

and so-called intellectual activity, he just turns
colder. Then comes comments regarding our wast-
ing our lives, sarcasm . . . He lets us know his dis-
approval."

"I heard a cabin on the estate blew up the other
day, before I got here."

"Yes. My father's 'think house.' "

"How did it happen?"

"One of his ideas must have caught fire while he
wasn't watching."

"Why would the heat be on in the cabin this
time of year?"

"Was it?"

"And the front axle of his Jeep broke while he
was driving it?"

"It shouldn't have. That Jeep is almost new."

"And Doctor Wilson was gassed to death in the
laboratory this afternoon."

"Do you suppose it was because he is an Afro-
American?"

"What would that have to do with anything?"

"Got me."

"Why would a physicist have lethal gas in his
laboratory anyway?"

She said, "I doubt he did."

Jack hesitated. "The lab blew up. I was there.
We all thought your dad was in the explosion. I
mean, dead. Killed by it."

Fixing her hair with her fingers, Alixis said:
"Oh."

"He looked rather heroic walking out of the

smoke carrying Doctor Wilson's body in his arms."

"Oh, that's just Dad," Alixis said. "Put him in a briar patch, and he'll just smell of roses."

"Does it seem to you someone just might be trying to kill your dad?"

Alixis shrugged. "I should care?"

He watched her flat eyes as she yawned. "Don't you?"

"Not really."

"He's your father."

"It would be nice not to be so pushed."

" 'Pushed' . . ."

"He bothers me a lot about what I'm doing, not doing."

"You starred in a movie?"

"That was finished late last summer."

"That must have been fun."

"It wasn't. Hanging around a film set is about the most boring thing you can do. It's all hurry up and wait."

"So you're an actress. You want to act."

"No. All that was my father's idea as something I should do. It's very important to him to report to the world what a great success each of his children is."

"Maybe it's important to him that each of his children is fulfilling himself."

" 'Himself' being him, you mean?"

"Why would he set up a movie for you to star in if—"

"I flunked out of Ol' Miss. What a disgrace. As

if I were the only person in the whole world who flunked out of college. I don't like school. It's too much work. Always having assignments hanging over your head. I mean, when you don't do the work, the teachers can get right nasty, as if it's any of their business. Why should they care if you don't do your work?"

"Why, indeed."

"So my father decided I should star in a movie. I had played Peter Pan once, in a school play. I wasn't very good, didn't like it much, but he insisted I was wonderful. He had this idea for a movie, got someone to write the script, hired a director—three directors, actually, before we were done. The first two quit. Said I wasn't cooperating. He spent these tons of money, bribed people to put the movie in their theaters, all to distract people from the fact that I hadn't cared to complete my college assignments. I guess he thought making a movie would turn me on, you know, as if I had a switch somewhere."

"Did you at least try to get into it, I mean, get enthusiastic, involved?"

"How can you get enthusiastic with everybody telling you what to do twelve hours a day? I had to work with a dance coach, singing coach, do things over and over until I was bored out of my mind. Rehearsing didn't do any good. I was never any better after I practiced something than before. It was all corny anyway. It was almost as bad as a children's story. 'Little Red Riding Hood' or something. Well, it came out last April, and everyone trashed it. They knew my father had bought and paid for it. They trashed me, as if it had been something I wanted to do. It wasn't my idea. I tried to tell them. They said I was the spoiled daughter of a rich man. The money should have been spent any other way, shelter the homeless, feed the hungry. Or to make a good movie with talent that would appreciate the opportunity. I was very embarrassed. I've hardly left Vindemia since. See what I mean by always being pushed? Who needs it?"

"What do you like to do?" Jack asked.

For the first time a light came into her eyes. She breathed through slightly parted lips. "Sex. I really like sex." She looked into Jack's face, at his neck. "You like sex?"

"Sure."

"I mean, it's the greatest thing. If you can play at sex, why would you do anything else?" Alixis wet her lips with her tongue. "Why isn't that enough for anyone? Everything else just takes energy I'm happier spending on sex."

The girl was getting warmer.

"Ah." Jack stood up. "I guess I better go over and see what needs doing to clean up the gym."

"Oh." She looked down at her tanned knees. She swung her legs back and forth from the bench, watching her muscles work.

Jack swept the clay court and then went around picking up the balls, putting them in their net bag.

She remained on the bench, watching him, swinging her legs.

When he returned, Alixis said, "Guess I should go, too. So I can mention I spent some time in the gym this afternoon."

"Hey, fatstuff," Alixis said.

The young man did not speak. He glanced angrily at his sister.

He was way overweight, soft-looking. His skin was sallow.

The four of them came together entering the gym. The two men wore greasy overalls, work boots. They had gotten out of a tow truck.

"This is my brother Duncan," Alixis said. "Jack Someone-or-Other." Duncan looked at Jack's uniform shorts and did not speak or offer to shake hands.

Jack had shifted the three tennis racquets to the hand carrying the net bag of tennis balls.

"The man who helps Duncan waste money on cars," Alixis drawled. "Alfred?"

"Albert," corrected Albert.

"And on other things. What are you goin' to do, brother? Surely not exercise."

"Take a steam."

"No, Duncan." Alixis sounded genuinely stern.

Jack wondered if Duncan's eyes were characteristically angry.

"Duncan," Alixis said, "you're full of shit. I can tell. You always are full of shit. Going into a steam room in your condition might kill you."

"So?" Duncan opened the door for himself. "Who cares?"

"You could have a heart attack." Alixis followed him through the door. "An aneurysm."

"Shut up."

"If you exercised instead of using that stuff—"

Duncan turned on his sister. "Shut your damned mouth."

"—and then you'll take more shit later."

Followed by Albert, Duncan went through a swing door.

Alixis said, "I don't care. Go kill yourself!"

Jack was looking for someplace to put the tennis equipment. There was a closet door. He opened it. Inside were more tennis equipment, basketballs, a volleyball set . . . All the equipment appeared new, unused.

Alixis said, "The boxing-wrestling room has a door on it that locks."

"What?"

"You know what I mean. We were talking about it."

Jack's heart raced. "What were we talking about?"

"Sex."

"You and me?"

"I don't see anyone else around."

"No," Jack said. "Not now. Maybe later. I have work to do."

"You agreed!"

"I did?"

"Oh, fuck you!" she said. "Go fuck yourself!"

"I work here," Jack said.

"I don't think I like you at all, Jack!"

"Sorry."

"Fuck off!"

"I knew you know that word."

Forearms crossed, she walked away from him, through the main glass doors into the sunlight.

She did have gorgeous legs.

"I need another six hundred and fifty thousand dollars!" Over the sound of the steam, people are apt to talk louder than they know in a steam room. They think they can't be heard outside their tiled room through the thick wooden door. "I've told the old man that, time and again! Why doesn't he just give it to me?"

Jack had checked the equipment in the weight room. No parts needed replacing. Put the free weights in their rack. Vacuumed the rug. The full length, full width mirrors on the walls did not need cleaning. He dry mopped the floor of the basketball court. Vacuumed the whirlpool.

As he went around the gym building he picked up dirty towels, few of them still wet.

The laundry cart was outside the steam room's door.

"He told me to write a proposal," Duncan scoffed. "Can you imagine that? Me? write a proposal? for a measly six hundred? So I did. You know what he did, the bastard? He corrected my spelling in red ink and sent it back to me."

"Should have used a word processor," Albert said. "They have Spellers."

"I did. I didn't use the Speller. I was in a hurry. The bastard! No other comment! Not yes, not no. Who does he think I am?"

Duncan and Albert had left all their greasy clothes on the floor of the corridor outside the steam room. There was no evidence they had showered.

"How much you already spent on the cars, Dunc?"

"Altogether? Not much. Million, million and a half." Albert said nothing. "Well, I won in Utah!"

"The mirror car was the only car in its class."

"Well, I won, didn't I?"

"You won."

"I mean, there's no point in getting into racing unless you're willing to spend the money. That's understood."

"Six hundred and fifty thousand dollars seems like a lot of money," Albert said. "To me."

"Not to my father. I don't have his support at all. Every time I see him, he asks me what business schools I've applied to. Everything is what he wants me to do, not what I want to do."

"What business schools have you applied to?"

"None."

"I thought you had."

"I lied."

"He wants you to learn Business Administration so you can help him out."

"Who cares about his business? He built it; he can suffer for it."

"It pays the bills."

"There's enough money so no one needs to work at it. No one needs to work at anything. Discipline! I'm disciplined."

"Sure," Albert said. "Ingest and press the pedal to the metal."

"I graduated from Vanderbilt, didn't I? He wanted me to do that."

"Yeah." Sorting towels, Jack heard Albert chuckle. "You hired other people to take your exams."

"Well, I graduated, didn't I? That's what he wanted. Now I want to improve the car I've got, two versions of it. I'm already signed up for a dozen races through this year, and I don't have the perfect car for it."

"You've got a great car. It almost gets away from you now."

"I can handle it. What am I gonna do?"

"Use some of your own money? What, he gave you ten million in stock on your twenty first birthday?"

"Why should I spend my own money? The Radliegh Mirror Car, I call it. My father should pay. It's good advertising. Anyhow, we're not supposed to sell the company's stock. I will, though, if I have to."

"The mirror car is blinding. To the other drivers. It shouldn't be allowed."

"I have other things to do with my own money."

"Stick it up your nose."

"Stick it up your ass."

"Go ahead. I'd know what to do with it. Get away from this crazy place. From you."

Jack wheeled the towel basket into the laundry and put the towels into the industrial-sized washer.

He planned to ride back to the village later and use the pay phone.

The idea of calling his father pleased him. He had never been able to do so until recently.

He had always felt the general need for his father.

Now he felt a specific need.

What would his father think of all this?

10

"**W**ant a beer?"

The young man who lived in the apartment next to Jack, in the same cottage, stood in Jack's door with two unopened cans of beer in his hands.

Jack had said "Hi" to him when they both arrived back from work shortly after five. Jack was bracing his bike in the stand.

Opening the door to his apartment, the other young man had said: "Fruity bikes."

He was wearing boots, jeans, and a checked white and blue shirt.

There was no other bike in front of that cottage.

"Sure," Jack said. "I'll have a beer."

"My name's Peppy."

He was a tall, lean young man with clear, naturally dark skin and curly dark hair.

"Jack," Jack said. "Where'd you get the beer?"

"From the duffel bag under my bed." Grinning, Peppy popped one beer can and handed it to Jack.

"I buy a week's supply on my day off. It's not cold."

"It's warm."

"So?" Peppy popped his own can and swallowed half the beer in it. "It's beer." He belched.

With the door open behind Peppy, a light breeze coming in, Jack smelled animals.

"What do you do with the empties?"

"Put 'em back in the duffel. Take 'em back to town with me when I go."

"People at the car compound don't notice you're carryin' a duffel bag that clanks?"

"I hide it in the bushes. Pick it up on the way out; drop it off on the way back."

"You smuggle beer."

"Yup," Peppy said. "You find yourself doin' some ridiculous things, around here."

Jack sat on the Hide-A-Bed couch. "You work in the stables?"

"How'd you guess? Because I smell of horseshit? That's my natural odor. My pappy smelled the same way." Peppy sat in one of the two white wooden chairs at the round table near the front window of the one-room-and-bath apartment. "I work the horses. Clean stables. Shovel shit. Want some?"

"Naw," Jack said. "I've got some hamburger for supper."

"Same shit."

"How many horses are there?"

"Eighteen now."

"That many?"

"Mostly unused. The old man rides. One or two of the young executives trying to attract his attention ride. Real dudes. You should see the one Japanese vice president of something or other ride. His head wobbles around so much, I swear it will fall off. You can tell he hates riding, poor guy; thinks it's somethin' he has to do for the glory of Radliegh Mirror, or somethin'. The old man tries to organize trail rides once in a while but he hardly ever can get any of his family to go. Chet's been riding, recently. You know? He put me on this place. Guests occasionally ride, some of them real good. I have to exercise the horses every day, clean them up again, do it again the next day, keep them gentle. You find yourself doin' some ridiculous things, around here. You ride?"

"No. But, if you like to ride, it seems like a good job."

"Lonely," Peppy said. "Never been lonelier in my life. Nobody, nothin' around here, either. Growing up, Oklahoma, I lived with horses, slept with them. Can't get away from them. I guess I am one, after all."

"One what?"

"A horse."

"How long you been here, on the place?"

"Three months. Four. Five. I have to be someplace. Do somethin'."

"Where did you meet Chet?"

"In a bar. In New York City."

"Not a good place for a horse, I think. What were you doing there?"

Peppy didn't answer at first. "Trying to get away from horses? Trying to stop being a horse? Trying not to be lonely?" Peppy turned his big-eyed long face toward Jack. "I look like a horse, don't I? I move like a horse."

"I don't know."

"I am a horse." Peppy tipped the beer can against his lips. "Neigh."

Jack wondered how much beer Peppy had drunk.

"I hear a horse died the other day."

Peppy nodded. "Under the old man. Dead before it hit the ground. Nearly rolled over on him. If the old man hadn't been quick, it would have broke his leg for sure."

"That all?"

"What do you mean?"

"Just broken his leg?"

"If the old man had been ridin' hard, jumpin' fences as he usually does, it could have killed him. 'Least he hasn't been back."

"Who?"

"The old man. Doc Radliegh. Hasn't ridden since. That surprises me. I thought the old man would be back the next morning lookin' to ride one of the other horses. He has eighteen of them left. But, no. Still, I'm there at the stables every mornin' with a horse saddled, ready for him."

"And he hasn't showed up?"

"No."

"Why not? Did the horse dyin' on him scare him, do you think?"

"In a way, maybe." Peppy shrugged. "He's doin' less of everything these days. His Jeep nearly threw him too, I hear. All his toys are breakin'. He's spendin' more of his time in his office, his lab."

"His lab. blew up this afternoon."

"That so?"

"Someone got killed there. A Doctor Wilson."

"I'll be damned. Another explosion?"

"Lethal gas. Then an explosion."

"I'll be damned. The old man's gettin' more and more corralled, ain't he? Damn near hobbled, I'd say."

"What was wrong with the horse?"

"Not a damned thing. It just keeled over. They're talkin' about it havin' a heart attack, but it didn't."

"You sure?"

"Well, it could have," Peppy said. "But that horse had more wind than any of 'em. It never had been short of breath, unduly. He could go straight up a steep hill and then break into a full-blown run. Which is why the old man liked him. Never had the slightest pain in his forelegs. Three years old."

"Was the horse killed, do you think? Poisoned, or something?"

"Something," Peppy said. "We'll never know. I was told to get that horse buried before I ever pissed again."

"A good horse like that," Jack said. "I don't

know. I'd think the old man would want an autopsy done on it. Him."

"Me, too. Always a chance of a virus, or somethin', affect the other horses. We'd need to know about it. No, sir: 'Bury that horse before it's cold, Peppy,' is what the old man said. So that's what I did. You find yourself doin' some ridiculous things, around here."

"So Doctor Radliegh has never gone back to the stables for his morning ride. You think someone is tryin' to get him, Peppy?"

"Doc Radliegh?" Peppy drained his beer can. "You'd have to be a fool not to suspicion it, wouldn't you say?"

"Is anybody doin' anything about it? Why doesn't he get out of here?"

Peppy shrugged. "What do I know? I'm just a horse."

"You got any ideas who might have poisoned the horse?"

"Anybody could have. Nothing is locked around here. Haven't you noticed?" Peppy pointed at Jack's front door. "There isn't even a lock on your own front door. Sure hope you left your diamonds to home."

"We're not safe in our beds."

"You got that right."

"Who around here would know how to poison a horse?"

"Anybody. Poisonin' a horse ain't difficult. Horses are poor, stupid critturs, like us. They can kick ya', throw ya', break your leg against a fence rail, but they ain't got no defenses against what you really can do to them, any time, all the time."

A large form blotted the sun out of the doorway. Against the light, Jack could not see who it was.

"I want a ridin' lesson," a man's voice said.

Peppy stood up. "Yes, sir, Caballero."

"Bareback." The man giggled.

"That takes a good horse," Peppy said. "One who won't throw ya."

Jack got up and crossed the room so he could see who was in the doorway.

"You get obstreperous," Chet drawled. "I'll just pull down on your ears."

He lunged at Peppy. He grabbed him by the ears. He pulled his head down. He raised his own knee. Gently he nuzzled Peppy's nose against his own thigh muscle.

Chet laughed and let go of Peppy. "Come on." He returned to the door. He said to Jack, "You want to join us?"

Red-faced, Peppy took Jack's beer can from his hand. He tried to crush a can in each hand simultaneously. Jack's half-full can squirted beer on the floor. "Oops! Sorry."

Chet had gone next door.

Peppy said, "You find yourself doin' some ridiculous things, around here."

Through the wall, Jack heard Chet and Peppy making noise in the next apartment.

Jack stuffed his swimsuit in a pocket of his shorts and went for a bike ride.

He rode past the office building, the airport, then around a nine hole golf course.

In the early dusk there were lights on in the clubhouse. There were a few expensive cars in the parking lot.

There was neither music nor laughter coming from the clubhouse.

From it, he could smell food cooking, especially fish.

Around the greens were executive style homes, with driveways, set deep in perfect landscaping.

These houses were more different from each other than were the smaller houses around Vindemia Village.

He biked up the long slope the other side of Vindemia's Main House. At the top of the hill, he stopped. Legs straddling his bike, he looked around. He believed the roof of the house was five acres. He counted ten enormous blue and white flags flying from tall poles on various places on the roof. Even in a light breeze the huge flags made a whipping sound.

He heard the murmur of talk.

Jack looked down into a large, square trellised garden heavy with roses red, yellow, white, even blue. He could see no one.

Still straddling it, he walked his bike forward a few steps.

On a bench in the garden sat a man and a woman.

The man was Doctor Radliegh.

As he talked, he held the woman's hand with both his hands in his lap.

The woman was Shana Staufel.

She looked up at Jack. After a moment, she smiled at Jack.

The man did not appear to notice him.

Jack sat on the bike seat and pedaled on.

In the village of Vindemia, Jack walked through the Recreation Center building. In the main lounge, a teen-aged boy and girl were playing Ping-Pong. Younger children sat along one wall playing computer games. Four teen-agers sprawled in couches looking at a huge television screen playing a music video not loudly.

None of the youngsters seemed to notice him.

Outside, on the veranda, two couples sat together in blue rocking chairs. On a blue wicker table were four tall glasses of what appeared to be iced tea.

They looked at Jack as he passed by them, but did not speak.

He was not sure they had been conversing with each other.

He changed into his swimsuit and alone swam in the huge, lit pool.

11

"**Y**ou see," Fletch said to Crystal from his lawn chair, "my father was thought to be emotionally evasive. I guess that mixes up my feelings about Jack, and, you. That you didn't let me know he existed, that I didn't know Jack existed until two weeks ago tonight ... leaves me uncertain as to how to respond to him."

"Your father died in childbirth," Crystal said from inside the handicap van. "So you always said."

"Not quite," Fletch said.

"He didn't?"

"He didn't."

It was after dark.

The van was in the parking lot of a motel near the room Fletch had taken for himself.

Inside the van, its side and back doors open to catch the breeze, Crystal sat propped up in her hospital bed.

Outside the van, on the pavement, Fletch sat in

a cheap metallic lawn chair.

A few people walking to and from their rooms and vehicles had looked at this odd arrangement of a man sitting in a chair on the pavement having a picnic with a woman propped up in bed in a van but none had said anything.

Crystal and Fletch had shared a supper of buckets of fried chicken, cartons of potato salad, coleslaw, large cups of iced tea.

As they drove West to Wyoming, Fletch had found it a bother stopping frequently to buy fast food for Crystal. She would complain of hunger just minutes after she had eaten more than he might in a week. He did not consider it his place or expertise to curb her eating, or even comment on it, but he remained amazed at the amount of food she consumed. He felt his unsolicited comments, efforts to restrain her would do no good anyway. It would just hurt and cause her to suffer the more.

With her, he found himself eating more. Just driving, not getting any real exercise, he was uncomfortable with undigested food constantly in his stomach. He felt sluggish, sleepy. As he drove he became more aware of his stomach against his belt, and he did not like that feeling.

Much more of a bother was having to stop at rest areas and help Crystal off her bed, out of the van, using the hydraulic lift, to the women's room so Crystal could relieve herself. The van had inadequate facilities for such functions. Never before had

Fletch realized what a long walk it was from most car parks to the lavatories. Her full weight of over six hundred pounds would lean on Fletch as Crystal swung one fat thigh around her other, stop a moment, sweating and panting, quivering with the exertion of taking a step. People, especially other women and children, would stare at them in amazement, scorn. Crystal's cheeks would be wet with tears at her humiliation. Breathing hard, she would say, over and over, "Fletch, how did I get this way? How did I get this way?"

Always on the long, torturous walks, Fletch would scan the other travelers for a strong looking woman with a touch of sympathy in her look. Such a woman he would ask to escort and help Crystal through the use of the women's room. Some just nodded their heads, "No," looked away, and went about their own business.

At the motel he had stayed in the night before, he had had to help her in and out of his bathroom evening and morning and help her through the entire routine himself. He tried to make light of it, but he certainly had not enjoyed it.

Fletch had always had great love for the human body and quietly remained horrified and depressed by seeing so closely what could happen to it by mere misuse.

So Fletch was sleeping in motel rooms these two warm nights on the road, Crystal in the van where she was more comfortable. She had read much of the previous night, snacking from bags of useless, greasy food he had bought at a truck stop for her.

Other than these botherations he was having a fine trip. As Fletch drove the van along America's good highways, he talked about everything under the sun with Crystal in her bed in back. Their heads were less than a meter away from each other, although Crystal was facing backward and had to repeat some things she said.

They talked about Jack. Fletch was full of questions about his son. Crystal's answers were detailed, incisive, understanding, frequently witty, admiring of her son, and, most of all, loving.

They talked about places they had worked as journalists, stories they had done, people they had known.

Fletch had many characters he had known, studied, resolved as much as one ever can, saved for "the long ride," as he had always called it, and this was a long ride, and he described many of them to Crystal.

"You mean, your father wasn't dead?" Crystal asked.

"No," Fletch said. "My mother only said that. I guess she thought it would make things easier for me."

"And did you actually meet him?"

"I ran into him, you might say."

"How interesting."

"I admit I was mildly curious."

Fletch's personal pocket communicator buzzed. He retrieved it from the front seat of the van.

"Hello?"

"Poppa! Poppa!" a child's voice cried.

"Oh, God," Fletch said, knowing it was Jack. "Not another one."

"Same one," Jack said in his own voice. "How's Momma?"

"Want to talk to her?"

"Sure."

While they talked, Fletch picked up all the wastepaper from their store-bought dinner and placed it in a nearby rubbish bin. Whether the American people realize it or not, Fletch thought, we are eating our trees.

"Fletch . . ." Crystal held the phone out to him.

Fletch took it and sat in his chair. He said: "Beep."

"When will you get Mom wherever you are taking her?" Jack asked.

"Tomorrow." He did not say he was not sure he could leave her there, in Mister Mortimer's boxing camp. In his heart, he knew his best idea was crazy.

"I'm wondering . . ."

"I should hope so."

"There are weird things going on here."

"At Vindemia?"

"Yes."

"That's why you went there, isn't it?"

"I'm at the pay phone outside the Vindemia Village General Store."

"I'm in a motel parking lot in Wyoming. So what?"

"I think there have been at least five attempts on Chester Radliegh's life, possibly six. One really misfired and murdered someone else, this afternoon."

"Who?"

"A scientist working in his lab."

"So talk to me."

"First Doctor Radliegh's three-year-old horse, one he uses to jump over things?"

"A jumper. Yes."

"Keeled over dead on him in the stable yard or whatever you call it."

"Means nothing. Whatever you least expect a horse to do, it will do. In fact, there is a strain of horse, beautiful horse, which at about that age will die of sudden heart seizure."

"The stableman thinks the horse may have been poisoned."

"Okay. What does the autopsy report say?"

"Doctor Radliegh wouldn't allow an autopsy."

"That's the first thing you've said that doesn't make sense."

"A wet, bare wire he would have to plug in to get his morning coffee was left in a dark place for him. He only happened to notice the wire was wet and bare."

"We're all booby-trapped by our friendly household appliances."

"His personal, in-his-dressing-room coffeepot unplugged, the wire wet, and bare, at dawn?"

"He could have rigged that himself."

"A cabin he was expected to be in alone at four o'clock in the afternoon blew up at four fifteen."

"Ummm. Is he having that investigated?"

"I think not. There's some silly explanation being passed around about the furnace blowing up."

"Maybe it did."

"A cabin furnace on in Georgia in the summertime?"

"Probably all of a piece with the air conditioning system."

"The front axle of a new Jeep he was driving on a mountain road broke."

"It could have been damaged."

"And," Jack continued, "after a Doctor Jim Wilson was killed by lethal gas in the laboratory, while Doctor Radliegh was in the lab, trying to rescue him, the lab blew up big-time. I was there. I saw it. I was sure Radliegh was killed."

"The gas hit some flame, a pilot light . . ."

"Why the delay? It wouldn't have taken that long for the gas to hit a flame in the same building. Why would a physicist have lethal gas in his lab. anyway?"

"Who knows? Undoubtedly Radliegh is playing with all sort of ideas, things no one knows about."

"Dad . . ."

Fletch felt a cool breeze. It made him shiver. "It does sound as if he's having a considerable run of bad luck. Did he break one of his own mirrors, do you suppose?"

"What Shana said is correct. There is reason for

me to be here. I think this guy is going to get killed."

"What about you? Are you being careful?"

"Oh, yes. No one suspects me. I've got a job as pool ornament."

"As what?"

"I take care of all the sports stuff, pools, tennis courts, gym. I'm being paid more than I'm worth."

"That's good."

"But I'm too far removed. I've only seen Radliegh twice. We haven't met. I can't protect him. I can't find out what's really going on."

"What have you found out so far?"

"He's built a paradise here in Georgia for himself, family, employees. They're safe, secure, have everything in the world they could want."

"Sounds nice."

"They're spoiled, at least his kids are, more than I ever believed possible."

"Of course."

"They hate him."

"Sure."

"More than hate. Resent him. Resent his existence."

"You think one of his kids is trying to do the old man in?"

"On the other hand," Jack said, "Doctor Radliegh appears to demand total control over everybody, where, how they live, what they're doing, saying, thinking, every minute, even what they eat and drink. I was told I had six minutes to drive from

the estate's front and only gate to the car compound to have my car locked up."

"Your car? You have a car? Of your own?"

"I bought one. In Virginia."

"What is it?"

"A Miata. A used Miata."

"Phew. Global Cable News must have overpaid
you, too. I'll have a word with Alex Blair about that.
Affects my dividends, don't you know."

"I believe Shana was right. Somebody is trying
to knock off Chester Radliegh."

"Shana is the girl who is going to marry young
Chester?"

Jack hesitated. "I'm not sure she's going to marry
him."

"Oh? Has the vision of you arriving in your two-
seater chariot rediverted her heart?"

"I think she's misread at least one thing here."

"I think I'm putting two-point-three and two-
point-three together—"

"—and coming up with five, I hope? Right.
Would you think of coming here to Vindemia?"

"Ain't been invited."

"You have to admit these are too many coincidences."

"There are a lot."

"And you are more a peer of Chester Radliegh."

"Little ol' me? A peer of the man who invented
the perfect mirror? You think I invented the rasp-
berry maybe?"

"Come on, Dad. I'm just a kid." Come on, Dad.

I'm just a kid. There was that cool breeze again. Fletch shivered. "What do I know?"

"Your mother comes first." Fletch felt noble in the saying.

"I'm trying to prevent a murder here and I don't think there's a whole lot of time."

"I'm just not sure," Fletch said. "We'll just have to see how things work out."

"Okay," Jack said. "Wish Mama mal apetite."

Fletch said, "Don't break any mirrors."

"Fletch?" It was later in the evening. Crystal and Fletch, sleepy now, were still keeping each other company in the parking lot of the Besame Motel. They heard a dance band playing from somewhere in the motel. They weren't dancing. "What's the difference between fat people and slim people?"

Fletch said, "Fat people have more weight?"

"Answer me seriously. It doesn't really have anything to do with big bones. My bones aren't big. Or glands. Surgery could fix that."

"Genetic proclivities?"

"No one in my family I ever heard of was fat. Not like me."

Fletch said, "I think it may have something to do with what one puts in one's mouth. Do you suppose?"

"I know that. But why do you put what you put in your mouth and I put what I put in my mouth?"

"I'm not comfortable feeling full of food. I guess you are."

"I see that. You hate having all this food and greasy bags around the van, don't you? Every time you open food parcels you've gotten for me, you sort of wrinkle your nose."

"I do?"

"You do. You wrinkle your nose and look away. Why does food that looks good to me repel you?"

"Habits, I guess. Just what we're used to."

"It's more than that."

"I once heard a famous professor of nutrition at Northwestern say something about people having to set or reset something like a food thermostat in their heads."

"What does that mean?"

Fletch said, "You become more accurately aware of what food you need to get along and only consume that much, no more. You eat high-energy food, the food that creates its own energy causing you to use it up, burn it off, with activity. You don't eat food that weighs more than the energy it produces. Something like that." The throbbing engine of an eighteen wheeler at the back of the parking lot was keeping time with the dance band. "I don't know. Why ask me?"

"I've asked enough experts."

"Paying for advice doesn't guarantee much."

"Fletch? Am I mentally ill?"

"Crystal, you're one of the brightest, most logical people I've known."

"Then why am I the way I am? What's logical about the way I eat? What sense does it make?"

"I don't know."

"I mean, what do slim people know that fat people don't?"

"I think slim people do know something."

"Please tell me what."

"I think slim people define hunger differently. I think slim people know that much of what you think of as hunger they realize is a food hangover. Have you ever noticed that when you eat more than usual you feel hunger pangs sooner?"

"Oh, yes. All the time."

"I think when you eat more than usual the body produces more than usual gastric juices, or something, and when they get done working on the food that is in the stomach, they send a signal to the brain saying they're ready for more food to work on. I think maybe fat people see that as a hunger pang. Slim people feel the same thing but know they're not hungry because they know they've eaten more than they need already."

"Hunger I feel is not real?"

"No. It's false. You just believe it's real."

"I'm not really hungry?"

"You can't be."

"Have you read this somewhere?"

"No. Just many times I've had to ignore hunger and discovered that the first hunger pangs aren't real. They mean nothing."

"The Chinese food syndrome."

"One is apt to overeat Chinese food. Therefore, an hour later one has hunger pangs. But one doesn't really need more food."

"So how do you know when you're really hungry?"

"You know. Your energy levels begin to drop. Then you should eat real food, not sugar, to maintain your energy. You should know about how much of what kind of food you need to produce the energy you need every day, and eat that much."

"And forget about the feeling of hunger."

"Something like that. I don't know what I'm talking about. I've been thinking about this, driving along, thinking about you. Maybe there are psychological reasons you are the way you are, as there are with everybody. I know you're not crazy. But a lot of the problem may be in your head. A misperception of what you're feeling. It's what that professor said about thermostats."

"Foodstats."

"Something like that. We think about food differently. Like people who drink more than usual and then get up in the morning and respond to the hangover by having more to drink. It doesn't make sense. One doesn't need more to drink just because the liver or whatever is ready to process more."

"Hunger pangs are a food hangover," Crystal said. "Now I've heard all."

"You asked. I'm no better than you. I just think about food differently."

"Maybe because you've been really hungry."

"Maybe."

"I wonder if I've ever been really hungry in my life."

"Probably not."

"I just feel hungry all the time."

"It's not hunger."

"Maybe you should write a diet book, Fletch."

"You think I could sell it?"

"Nothing sells better than diet books. Diet books and cookbooks."

"I don't know anything about it."

"That's never stopped other people from writing diet books."

"I've just been thinking about it. About you. For you, maybe."

His pocket communicator buzzed. He picked it up off the pavement beside his chair. "Hello?"

"Fletch, Mister Mortimer called here again."

Fletch said to Crystal, "It's Carrie, calling from the farm."

"Your lover," Crystal said. "Give her my best. No, come to think of it, she already has my best."

Carrie said, "He sounds real mean, Fletch."

"Mister Mortimer is real mean," Fletch agreed.

"He's warning you off his place loud and clear. How close are you to his boxer training camp, or whatever it is, now?"

"Pretty close. Another three hours, maybe. We should be there by nine or so in the morning."

"Fletch, he doesn't want you."

"Sure he does. Everybody likes me. I've told you that."

"He hates you!"

"He just forgets."

"He insists you ruined his life."

"How could I have done that? I just got him to put all his friends in jail, that's all. Why should he be upset about that?"

"Then he had to run for his life, he tells me. From the boxing world to cow heaven, he says. From New York City to Wyoming, which he hates or doesn't understand, or both. He's lonely, angry, bitter—"

"And mean. I know all that."

"Fletch, this is the seventh or eighth time he's called here, warning you off. You should hear him talk!"

"I have."

"I think you'd better take him seriously."

"I do."

"It's a crazy idea, anyway, taking an overweight lady to a boxers' training camp."

"I've had crazier ideas," Fletch said, "that have worked out."

"Fletch, he's said he's borrowed three shotguns from neighbors. That if you drive onto his place he and his two boys—"

"Haja and Ricky."

"He says they're as mean as bare wires snappin' in a rainstorm."

"They're as tame as garden hoses."

"—will blast your head off."

"Boxers don't know how to aim beyond arm's length."

"Please, Fletch. He's serious, I swanee down the back."

"If he calls again . . ." Fletch hesitated.

"What?"

". . . tell him we'll be there about nine in the morning. Leave a lamp burnin' in the window, darlin'. I'll be home, either with my head on my shoulders, or carried under an arm, but I'll be there."

After he clicked off, Crystal said, "How much does Carrie weigh?"

"One hundred and twenty three pounds."

"You don't know how much I weigh, do you?"

"No."

"That's good."

12

"**W**ho—?"

Jack's head snapped off the pillow. In his dark bedroom he had been asleep on his stomach. His right leg was over someone else's legs. Those legs were muscular, and smooth. His right arm was over someone else's stomach. He withdrew his arm and propped up his shoulders by his elbows. He thought he had been dreaming. He had begun to move. He was primed. He slid his leg off the legs of the other person's. Holding himself up on one elbow, gently he felt the other person's breasts.

A naked girl had gotten into his bed with him.

He breathed hard. He listened to the low hum of the window air conditioner.

It had been weeks since a girl had been in bed with him.

After biking in the dark back from Vindemia Village he had played his guitar softly half an hour, thinking about his conversation with his father, about the previous weeks, setting the Tribe story up with the authorities, his five weeks in the maximum security prison in Kentucky, his time in the encampment in Alabama, his working day and night in Virginia, how confining Vindemia was.

He had been thinking about sex, how long it had been since he had loved anyone, anyone had loved him. Thinking about girls he had loved and who had loved him. Thinking about the when and where and how of some of the times he had made love. Wondering how in this life with people moving great distances continuously boys and girls, men and women got together, gobbled each other up, sometimes their minds and spirits as well as their bodies, given to each other, taken from each other, really loved and sometimes learned from each other, and then been separated by circumstances, families, schools, schedules, jobs, mobility, distances, no reasons romantic or usually even emotional. Perhaps because of practicalities, society's new lessons, through its courts, the centeredness on self in mental health practice, Jack's generation had been taught above all else that long-range relationships did not, would not work; one must not hope or even think of such.

So there were many of whom he thought, many missed, each once a swelling on his heart now a scar.

He ran his hand down the girl's body.

He said, "Shana?"

There was an explosion next to him in the bed.

The sheet was flung, kicked up into the air.

A fist pounded down hard on the muscle below his right shoulder blade.

A hand gripped the muscle of his right shoulder. Another gripped his right hipbone.

He was flipped over onto his back.

She sat on the base of his stomach.

She was slapping his head, face, shoulders with both hands.

In the dark he tried to find her flaying arms, grab them, protect his head.

Finally he crunched his stomach muscles, sat up enough to get his arms around her back. He pulled her down to him.

She straightened her legs along his.

He rolled over on top of her.

She stretched her legs wide, hustled him inside her, gripped her legs behind his back.

It continued violent and was sudden.

Letting out a long exhale, she said: "Alixis."

Then, almost immediately, she said: "More."

There was more.

He did not realize the skin of his back was torn until the shower's hot water hit it sometime later.

There was blood mixed with the water on the shower's floor.

After drying off, he twisted to see the length of the gash on his back in the bathroom mirror.

Then he was sitting on the edge of his bed.

Behind him, on the bed, Alixis asked, "Anything the matter with you?"

"You cut me."

"Oh, poor Jack." Instantly, in the dark, the tips of her fingers ran along the cut on his back. She had known she had cut him, exactly where.

The cut was sticky and made her fingertips sticky.

He was still bleeding a little.

"Poor you," she said. "Red blood. Red blooded boy."

"Just thinking," he said.

"What is poor bleeding boy thinking? Can't afford the blood? Do you mind losing it that much?"

"If I did to you what you just did to me, I'd be in prison for twenty years."

"Shit," Alixis said. "I'm not the first girl who's snuck into your bed while you were asleep and fucked your brains out."

"No," Jack said. "You're not."

"Boys like it any time, any place. Isn't that right?"

Jack didn't say anything.

"You all come with Everready batteries. I know that. I mean, you have it. You've got to give it. It's got to go some place. Isn't that true?"

He said, "Yeah."

"And you can't get pregnant."

"What are you talking about?"

"Girls have something long considered an asset,

something they can sell, give away, or not. It's their choice."

"And boys don't have a choice?"

"Not if a girl wants it. Boys are sexy. They produce and produce and produce. Onto the ground or into a girl. It's a girl's choice to take it or not."

"I see."

"Boys can't get hurt." She knelt on the bed behind him. She folded her arms around his chest. She put her cheek on the top of his head. "Did poor Jack get hurt?"

"You can't hurt a boy," Jack said, "is what you said."

"I'm sorry I scraped your back." Moving against him, she was smearing the blood dripping down his back onto her belly.

"It's all right."

"Does it hurt?"

"Stings."

"You shouldn't even complain about it."

"I'm not complaining."

"You can't say you didn't enjoy it."

"I enjoyed it."

"Boys always enjoy it."

"Sure," he said.

"Sure," she said. "Boys can't stop themselves. Good boys always enjoy it. Good boys are fucking machines. They're just there to be fucked. And what's also nice is that they never complain."

"No," Jack said. "Never."

She clutched his hair with her fingers and pulled

his head back, way back. Her other hand clutched his extended throat, his neck muscles, and squeezed.

Her lips found his mouth. She forced her tongue through his lips, his teeth, into his throat.

He had to twist toward her. Again he wrapped his arms around her arms, around her back.

Alixis said: "More."

There was more.

13

"**Y**ou have a cut on your back."

"Yes." While Jack was raking the Japanese garden, Radliegh's secretary, Nancy Dunbar, had come into the garden with a cup of coffee. She sat on the bench she and Jack had used the day before and lit a cigarette.

"Don't let it get sunburned," she said, "or you'll have a scar there forever."

"I know."

It was early Saturday morning. Jack was in the shade of the garden's wall.

"Do you have anything to tell me?" Nancy Dunbar asked.

His first time doing such a thing, Jack was trying to make an interesting design on the garden's sand with his rake.

Did he have anything to tell her? In Nancy Dunbar's words, "Any plans you hear anybody make; if you see people together you think don't belong together; comments you hear people make about each other, Mr. Beauville, me, Doctor Radliegh. . . ."

Only a few hours before, in the dark of his bedroom, he had found himself sucking his own blood from the tits of Doctor Radliegh's younger daughter.

Jack had heard that same daughter say she didn't care if her father was murdered; had heard Duncan Radliegh admit he had cheated to graduate from college, lied about applying to any business school, considered disobeying and selling stock in Radliegh Mirror to support his car racing interest and, Jack surmised, his drug habit.

He had seen the elder son, Chet, All-American quarterback, betrothed to Shana Staufel, demand sexual attention from the stableboy.

He knew there was a duffel bag full of beer under Peppy's bed.

He had seen Doctor Radliegh himself and Shana Staufel sitting on a bench in a rose garden at dusk talking quietly while holding hands.

He had heard local people mock Nancy Dunbar.

"No," Jack said. "Nothing."

"You've heard, seen nothing which might be of interest to us?" Nancy Dunbar asked.

"Nothing."

"You're making the design in the sand too tight," Nancy said. "Loosen up."

"Loosen up?"

"Yes. Relax with the rake. Use it as a paint-brush."

"I've never used a paintbrush," Jack said, "except to paint a garage."

"Think of an abstract painting," Nancy said. "Make big swirls, curves, straight lines at odd angles."

"Oh."

"You're too tight."

He started over. He didn't know what to do with the sand around the big, jagged rocks in the garden. He sensed the lines made by the rake's tines ought not dead-end at the rocks, but flow around them somehow.

"It's Saturday morning," Jack said. "Not even eight o'clock."

"Yes." Nancy lit another cigarette.

"You work every day of the week?"

"I'm supposed to have Saturday afternoons and Sundays off."

"Do you?"

"Maybe once a month. This isn't a job, it's a living. Doctor Radliegh's mind never stops. And when he wants something, he wants it right away. He himself keeps a very tight schedule, but he never really knows, or cares, what time of day it is, or even what day it is. It's a little hard to understand that, at first. It seems contradictory, doesn't it?"

"Is that all right with you?"

"That's fine with me. I am going to be able to

leave here someday reasonably young, and very rich."

"That's nice."

"By the way, there's a big party here tonight."

"You mentioned it."

"You're serving drinks, whatever."

"Drinks? Here? At Vindemia?"

"Of course. Chester can't dictate the habits of the whole world. Show up at the kitchens of the main house about five thirty. White shorts, dress white shirt. They'll give you a blue bow tie when you get there."

"Okay."

"Tell me anything odd you hear, see, tonight."

"Okay."

"In the meantime, you can take this afternoon off."

"Thanks."

"I mean, don't plan to leave Vindemia, in case somebody wants you. Like, go for a swim, or something."

Eric Beauville, dressed in plaid shorts and a pink short-sleeved shirt, stood in the arched gateway of the Japanese garden. He had a manila folder in one hand.

"No, you'd better not go for a swim," Nancy said. "You don't want that cut on your back to scar."

Beauville said, "A gardening accident?"

Jack said, "I got scraped."

"Sure," Beauville said. "Did the same tree give

you those hickeys on your neck and chest?"

Nancy Dunbar looked at Jack with narrowed eyes.

Laughing, Beauville sat on the bench next to Nancy. "I'm blessed by far-sightedness."

"Who—?" Nancy started to ask.

Beauville nudged her. "Gimme a cigarette."

She did so, and lit it for him.

"It's nice that ladies can carry purses," Beauville said, inhaling gratefully. "If old Chester ever spotted a package of cigarettes on me, he'd tongue whip me for weeks, and see that my health insurance premiums tripled." He took another deep drag. "Yet I don't seem to be able to get off this Goddamned place without an excuse from a doctor, which I can't get, because Chester's got a kept doctor on the estate."

Nancy said, "I thought you were to play in a golf tournament in Sea Island this morning."

" 'Were' is right." Beauville exhaled. "I were. Our inspired leader called me at five fifteen a.m. demanding a complete review of his Will, Estate, Trusts, cash in hand . . ."

"You mean 'Will,' " Nancy asked, "as in Last Will and Testament?"

"Last Will and Testicles," Beauville said. "Nicolson is flying in from Atlanta. Clarence is on his way here from Ronckton."

Jack asked them: "Am I supposed to disappear at this point?"

"Naw," Beauville said. "Without even checking,

I know you're not mentioned in the Will, What's-your-name."

Jack said, "That's a relief."

"I like the design you're making," Beauville said. "Nice and tight."

"Thanks."

"And you don't look a bit Japanese."

"Sorry."

"Too tight," Nancy said.

"That's what I can do to annoy Chester," Beauville said. "I can put the proposition to him seriously: If he has a Japanese garden, why doesn't he have a Japanese gardener? I'll hint he might be charged with discrimination."

Nancy said, "He'd take it seriously."

"I know he would. Someday I'd like to drive him as nuts as he drives me."

"You're not smart enough, Eric," Nancy said.

Beauville said, "I can try."

"What could he be thinking?" Nancy asked. "Why the rush review of his estate?"

Beauville extinguished his cigarette against the sole of his loafer. "Maybe Jim Wilson's being killed by lethal gas in a laboratory where there wasn't known to be any lethal gas yesterday has something to do with it." He handed his cigarette butt to Nancy.

"Jim must have been planning some experiments of his own." She put Beauville's cigarette butt into the Ziploc baggy in her purse. "Or someone else at the lab was."

"Sure," Beauville said. "There's an explanation for everything."

Dunbar said, "Things happen."

Beauville said to Nancy, "Chester didn't want me to play in that golf tournament this morning. He never wants me to leave Vindemia. He's afraid someone reasonable might make me an offer to run a reasonable company and live a reasonable way of life."

"You never would," Nancy said.

Beauville said: "In a heartbeat."

He stood up. "Come on. You have to help me get some papers out of one of the smaller, underground, bombproof safes."

She collected her purse and her empty coffee cup.

Looking at Jack's raked design in the sand, Beauville said, "It's gettin' too loose now. I liked it better before."

Scurrying after Beauville, Nancy Dunbar said, "It's still too tight."

14

"**H**ere we are," Fletch said. "I think."

There was no sign on the long, empty dirt road. There were just decayed fences extending out of sight on both sides of the road.

"Oh, joy," Crystal said from her bed in the back of the handicap van. "I finally get to meet Mister Mortimer, the meanest man in the world. Do you suppose he will hang me upside down by my toes?"

"He might." A half mile down the road on the left a few buildings were visible in the shade of a clump of deciduous trees. Fletch felt for Mortimer. This sparse country was a long way indeed from the noisy arenas of the northeast. He almost felt guilty. "He just might."

They were arriving at Mortimer's boxing camp even earlier than Fletch had thought. It was five past eight. Neither Crystal nor he had slept well. They had gotten on the road before dawn. They stopped only twice for food and not at all for lavatory facilities. The first person Fletch asked in the small Wyoming town gave immediate, simple directions to the boxing camp. The local citizen Fletch asked said, "You mean that mean son of a bitch New York bastard?" He knew just where Mortimer lived.

Fletch said, "He may hang us both up by the toes."

Fletch accelerated the van down the bumpy, dusty road.

"Fletch!" Crystal complained from the rear of the van. "You might bounce me off the bed!"

"I've decided to try to take the old bastard by surprise." Seeing the place, Fletch considered that Mortimer had real reason to shoot Fletch on sight.

"Fletch, slow down!"

"Hang on!"

"Are you sure you're doing the right thing bringing me here?"

"Of course not!"

"Help! Let me out!"

"Now, Crystal," Fletch said in a reasonable tone. "You wouldn't know you were in Wyoming without a rough ride."

A lanky old man appeared at the edge of the cluster of trees surrounding the buildings. In one hand was a shotgun. He fired into the air.

A shirtless boy in shorts ran to a position a few meters from Mortimer and knelt on one knee. He, too, carried a shotgun. He took aim at the van.

He fired.

A puff of dust arose in the air just in front of the van.

"Fletch!" Crystal screamed. "They're shooting!"

"They're shootin'," Fletch said, "but they ain't hittin'."

He began swinging the van's steering wheel. "Zigzag," he said.

"Fletch! Enough of zigzag! I'm sloshing around back here!"

Through the rearview mirror, Fletch saw the bottom half of Crystal's sheet rising into the air. She must be raising her legs, he realized.

He didn't know she could do that.

Mortimer, having reloaded, fired at the van.

His shot went high.

Fletch left the road. He aimed the van straight at Mortimer. He accelerated.

Going over ground even rougher than the road made the van jounce wildly.

"Fletch!" Crystal sounded like she was strangling. "You're beating me to death!"

Mortimer jumped out of the way.

Holding his shotgun by the barrel like a club, the boy ran after the van.

Fletch stopped the van near the buildings in the shade of the trees.

In the swirling dust, the boy stopped a meter from Fletch's open window.

"Hi," Fletch said through the window. "Are you Haja, or Ricky?"

"Ricky."

"What? Say that again."

"Ricky."

"Wow. 'Ricky.' "

"What is the matter?"

"Never heard anybody say that before, I guess. That way."

The sixteen year old had the perfect boxer's build.

But his voice had a timbre that sounded as if it were coming from the back of a miles-long cave.

Ricky, holding the shotgun by the barrel with one hand, gently rested its butt on the ground. He positioned his legs oddly, creating the impression of being totally alert and relaxed at the same time.

Chin tilted sideways, the boy's eyes looked at the ground between them. Then he ran his eyes slowly up the van's door and fixed them on Fletch's face.

Doing these simple things the boy gave the impression of complete readiness, to listen or to fight, to laugh or to twist Fletch's head off.

"Wow," Fletch said. "Fascinating."

Fletch was dimly aware of Mortimer stumbling up, yelling his head off.

He tuned Mortimer in. "—G.D. S.O.B.! I told you to stay a state's length away from me! I told you if you showed up here, I'd shoot you! And Goddamn it, I will!"

So great was Mortimer's fury that he dropped the shell he was trying to jam into the shotgun.

Another young man, heavily muscled and well over six feet tall and naturally darker than Ricky, stood under a nearby tree, his long arms relaxed at his sides.

Fletch said to him, "How're ya doin', Haja?"

"Good," Haja answered.

Fletch surmised from both boys' sweaty hair and dusty socks they had been on a long run.

He envied them.

While Mortimer was picking the shotgun shell off the ground, Fletch got out of the van.

"Dreadful lookin' place you got here," Fletch said. "It's a wonder we didn't give it back to the American natives."

As Fletch walked straight up to him, Mortimer dropped the shell again. He snapped the empty gun barrel closed. He pointed it at Fletch's stomach.

"I told that damned woman of yours who answers your phone in Tennessee that if you showed up here I'd blast your head off."

"Fletch?" Crystal's voice quivered from the back of the handicap van. "Fletch?"

"She's not a damned woman," Fletch said, "and she's not mine. She does answer the phone, when it rings. And I don't much appreciate a city foul-mouth like you shoutin' barnyard language at a genuine country lady long distance!"

Mortimer's eyes were blazing. "I'll be damned!" He flung the empty shotgun onto the ground. "I'll show these boys how I can take you apart with my fists!"

Fletch backed up. "Never mind. I suspect they know you can."

Mortimer's fists were raised. Wiry, at seventy-four, he was ready to rain every combination of punches all over Fletch.

"Relax," Fletch said. "I made you a hero."

"A hero!" Mortimer exploded. "To who?"

"To the world!"

"The only people I cared about in the world I put in prison, thanks to you!"

"They were bad guys, and you know it."

"They were my friends!"

Fletch turned his back on Mortimer's fighting stance. Through his nose he inhaled deeply. "Fresh air. Don't you just love it?"

"Fresh air!" Mortimer yelled. "What's it good for? It smells like nothing! You know how long it's been since I've smelled a bakery?"

Turning full circle, Fletch noticed Ricky had disappeared.

Haja still stood curious under the tree.

"I'll send you a loaf of Brooklyn pumpernickel," Fletch said. "You can stick it up your nose."

Lithe as a panther, Mortimer came swinging at Fletch. "I'll rip your nose off you!"

Not raising his hands, Fletch ducked and backed up. "Cut that out!"

Pursuing him with perfect footwork, Mortimer said, "I'll cut your fuckin' heart out! Your eyes—"

Backing up, Fletch's heel tripped on Mortimer's shotgun.

Fletch fell to the ground.

Resting on his elbows, Fletch said, "You can't hit me down here."

"Mister Mortimer?" Ricky's low voice demanded immediate attention.

He was standing in front of the van.

"Mister Mortimer," Ricky said. "Come here, please." His voice was as pervasive as mist. "There is something you must see."

Fists still at the ready, Mortimer studied the boy. "Can't you see I'm busy? I'm going to make chopped liver out of this . . ."

"Wuss," Haja said.

Mortimer looked down at Fletch on the ground. "He's a 'was' all right. He's a never was! Get up, you bug, you bugger, you journalist!"

"If I do, you'll hit me," Fletch said. "So what's the point? I'll only find myself down here again." .

Ricky: "Please, Mister Mortimer."

"All right." Mortimer aimed a not very serious kick at Fletch's boot. "What is it?"

He spat on the ground and stamped around the front of the van.

Fletch quickly got up and followed them.

Ricky had opened the sliding door on the other side of the van.

"What is it?" Mortimer asked impatiently.

Using his well-sculpted head as would a stag, his eyes as would a man who had looked from the top of mountains, Ricky indicated Mortimer ought look inside the van.

Mortimer looked. Then peered. Then squinted. "What is it?"

Crystal let out a little sob.

Mortimer stepped up into the van.

He looked a moment at Crystal on the bed.

He gasped.

"Oh, my dear lady!" He picked up her hand. "What has happened to you?"

"Oh, Mister Mortimer!" Crystal wept. "I don't know!"

"I'm glad you brought her here," Mortimer said. "Now get out."

He had come from behind Fletch, through the broken spring door of the old farmhouse.

Fletch, feeling shunted aside by all the activity, had been standing on the porch looking out over the plain. A Mrs. Robbins he had found in the kitchen had provided him with a cup of coffee.

He had driven through some gorgeous parts of Wyoming to get here, but these acres were desolate. It looked to him as if the grass grew here as thin hay. A cow by herself would need acres to graze. Here even a cow would be lonely.

Immediately upon discovering Crystal in the back of the handicap van Mortimer had begun organizing.

While Crystal waited in the van, Haja and Ricky had dismantled Mortimer's own king-sized bed and lifted its frame, box-spring and mattress to the barn and rebuilt it in a corner of the gymnasium just outside the swing door to the locker room. Mortimer made the bed himself.

The gym was not that large, but it was well built: hardwood floor, a boxing ring in the center, the latest in exercise machines along the far wall, as well as head and body punching bags.

The only thing odd about the gym was that the mirrors on the walls were old-fashioned: they were not perfect mirrors.

There was a sauna and whirlpool in the locker room, as well as open showers, basins and toilets.

Having some experience at it, Fletch tried to help bring Crystal into her new bed. Silently, firmly, Mortimer, Haja, Ricky elbowed him aside. They let Fletch run the van's hydraulic lift to lower them all to the ground.

On the porch, Fletch said to Mortimer, "You don't really hate me, do you?"

Mortimer spat over the porch rail. "Sure. You did the right thing, Fletch, as far as I was concerned. So did I. I'd seen what was wrong with the boxing game all my life, never took part in the filth but I went along with it. Impaling my young contender on that iron fence in Gramercy Park . . ."

"His name was Shane—?"

"Goldblum. Shane Goldblum. . . . Well, it made everything inside me, how can I say it, hunker down, atomize, and then . . ."

"I came along and gave you a way of blowing up."

"You see, with my friends in prison, well, when

we write back and forth to each other, I blame you for everything. Everything I did to them."

"They deserved it. They're bad guys."

"Yeah, but they're my bad guys. We grew up together, worked together. Who else, what else do I know? Loyalty may be a virtue, but it's also a convenience. So, yeah, I hate you. You made the best of me, so I hate you. What else do you expect? My best boxers came to hate me. I made the best of them, they'd find themselves unique, alone, isolated, just like I am, so they'd blame me, hate me. Most people, I figure, never do anything unusual, they just go along with whatever it is, mediocrity, corruption, because they can't stand the idea of being unique, alone, isolated." Mortimer's blue eyes scanned the field Fletch had just been watching. "I've been thinking of importing some pigeons. How do you think they'd do here?"

"Not well. Not enough used lunch bags."

"Yeah. Well, the place needs used lunch bags, too."

"Haja and Ricky seem like nice kids. Hopefully contenders."

"Sure."

"That Ricky has some presence."

"Presence?"

"You haven't noticed?"

"What's presence already?"

"I don't know. Dignity? His own sense of time, space, sight, sound? Self-awareness?"

"He's just in love with himself. Somehow he

makes you pay attention to him, watch him, when he's not doing anything! A boxer? I don't know."

"So you think you'll be able to help Crystal?"

"You said she's a heavyweight."

"Yes, I did."

"A heavyweight challenge all right."

Fletch said, "I'll go say good bye."

"You're leaving?" Crystal asked. "You're leaving me here?"

"Mister Mortimer is putting me off the place," Fletch said.

"Don't hesitate," Mortimer said.

"Where're you going?"

"Somewhere the landscape has more than one line to it."

"Get out of here," Mortimer said. "Ricky, see this bum off the place."

"I'll call," Fletch said to Crystal.

"Tell Jack where I am."

As Fletch was escorted by Ricky out of the gym, Mortimer was saying, "Now, listen, dear lady. You're not going to lose weight right away. First we're going to build you some muscle. You'll be losing fat, but you'll weigh the same, because muscle weighs more than fat, you see? So you're not to get discouraged."

Crystal murmured, "All I want is to take in the food I need for what I'm doing."

"That's very good," Mortimer said. "Where did you learn that?"

By the angle of his head, the way he used his arms and his legs, turned his body into a K closing the side door of the van, somehow Ricky made Fletch watch him do it.

Mortimer may have developed the kid's body but the kid's presence was as natural to him as the color of his hair.

Fletch said, "I notice you don't use contractions."

Ricky said, "I do not?"

He opened the van's door for Fletch.

"Bye," Fletch said.

"Good bye."

15

"**Y**ou there!"

Walking his bike on a gravel path skirting the side of Vindemia's main house, Jack looked up. An older woman was calling to him from a balcony. Wisps of her graying hair and her light bathrobe were being blown by the wind.

"Come here!" She pointed to an open, arched doorway beneath her balcony. "Go in there. Come up the steps."

Overhead the ten huge flags on the roof were snapping imperiously in the wind.

He leaned his bike against a wall, went through the arch and up the stone stairs in the wall of the house.

She was the woman he had seen possibly weeping in the back of the chauffeur-driven stretch Infiniti the day he arrived.

"Do I know you?" she asked him. "I mean, have we done this together before?"

"What?" Jack asked.

"I need someone to take out my rubbish," she said.

"Oh."

"People keep forgetting," she said. "To take out my rubbish."

"I see."

"I need this help."

"Okay."

"You look like the last boy who used to help me."

"We're infinitely replaceable," Jack said.

"I'm glad you realize that. He was my friend." She stuck a bill into the pocket of his shorts. "Will you be my friend?"

"Sure."

"It's just this bag over here." On the floor of the balcony near the French doors was a green garbage bag. "People keep forgetting it, you see."

"I see."

"If you'd just dispose of it for me."

"Sure." When he picked the bag up its contents clanked.

"That will be all." Looking straight ahead, she went through the French doors into the house.

Jack found the latticed yard behind the kitchen of the house where the many covered rubbish barrels were placed in wooden, hatched bins. The area was as scrubbed as a surgery.

Jack lifted the garbage bag into a barrel.

Then he opened the garbage bag.

Within were many vodka bottles, a few sherry bottles, port bottles, brandy bottles, all empty.

There were also many differently shaped pill vials, all empty. The names of the prescription drugs on the typed labels meant little or nothing to Jack. Instructions limited the number of each pill taken daily and usually recommended taking upon rising or at bedtime. They were prescribed by various doctors, MacMasters, Donovan, Harrison and Chiles.

All the prescriptions were for Amalie Radliegh.

Jack would have thought the woman had just cleaned out her medicine chest of years' accumulations, but all the dates on the prescription labels were within the last three weeks.

He retied the top of the garbage bag and closed the hatch.

Walking back to his bike, he took out the bill Mrs. Radliegh had stuffed into his pocket and looked at it.

It sure was an easy way to make $50.

16

"**A**re you marrying Chet?" Jack asked.

"Yes," Shana answered.

"Why?"

Jack had walked his bike down to the swimming pool and left it leaning against a wall.

Shana Staufel was swimming her laps.

Otherwise the pool area was empty.

Jack waited for her to finish. He sat in a chair in the shade of the wall nearest the house. He could not be seen there from any of the windows, balconies of the house which overlooked the pool generally. He had learned that trick from Nancy Dunbar regarding the office windows next to the Japanese garden.

A small jet airplane circled over Vindemia to land at the estate's airfield.

Shana had not seen Jack when she first came out of the water.

"Hey," he had said in a low voice.

Drying her head with a towel, she had walked over to him. Today she was wearing a yellow bikini which brought wonderful light to her skin.

Now sitting on a cushioned chair near Jack she said, "So you know about Chet."

"What do I know about Chet?"

She said, "He likes boys."

"Does he like girls, too?"

She shrugged. "No way, José."

"Then why are you marrying him?"

"It's an arrangement."

" 'An arrangement.' "

"Yes. Have you never heard of an arranged marriage?"

"A marriage of convenience?"

She nodded. "Very convenient."

"What's convenient about it?"

"There are certain ambitions," Shana said, slowly, carefully, "which easily can be realized. For Chet to pass the Bar Exam, practice law locally, briefly, run for United States Congress, first, then, you know . . ."

"Buy the hearts and minds of the American people."

"He's very bright. He'll be brilliantly staffed and advised. Already a book has been written for him contrasting the First and Fourteenth Amendments—"

"Written for him?"

"It will be published under his name. The ghostwriters have been well paid for both their work and their silence."

"That's nice."

"The District's present Congressman is expected to retire after this term."

"How old is he?"

"Late forties."

"Why is he retiring?"

"He'll have enough funds to do whatever he wants."

"Thanks to Chester Radliegh, Senior."

"Yes."

"He's being paid to retire. Bribed."

"Some people take their financial security very seriously. His congressional seat happens to be his major asset."

"Which he can sell."

"Yes."

"To Radliegh and son."

"Yes."

"Sure. The Congressman shouldn't sit on his asset. Whose ambition is this? Radliegh's, or son's?"

Shana sighed. "Chester believes strongly that what good can be done ought be done. With his father behind him, Chet can accomplish far more for this district, for the nation, maybe the world, than can the present incumbent."

"I daresay. So it is believed that for his political career Chet needs a savvy, presentable wife."

"You're lookin' at her."

"There are gay members of Congress now."

"Not from Georgia. Not at this time, there aren't," Shana said. "Sodomy laws have been removed from the books so recently here you can still see the dust from the eraser."

"If this is Doctor Radliegh's ambition, why is Chet going along with it?"

"Why not?"

"It means living a lie."

"It would be fun. Chet's very popular. All-American quarterback. Handsome. Bright. He's got to do something with his life. Can't live here playing Ping-Pong with his little sister all his life."

"He doesn't have to go into politics."

"It's what his father has always wanted. Chester is trying to shape Duncan up as the titular head, figurehead, whatever you want to call it, of the Radliegh business interests."

"Good luck to him."

"Yeah," Shana said. "Good luck."

"So Chet agrees to this marriage."

"Agrees? Yeah. He agrees. We like each other well enough. Why not? He's a bright, charming guy. As long as everything is understood. He gets to do what he wants, discreetly. This way Chet gets a degree of freedom, gets off Vindemia—"

"He'll never be his own man in Washington."

"Who ever is?"

"The Constitution expects a member of Congress to have a constituency of more than one."

"One genius like Chester is probably worth more

than the intellectual abilities of a sizable popula-
tion."

"So Doctor Radliegh knows his son is gay."

"Yes. This is the arrangement he has made for
his son."

"It's more than an arrangement. It's a deal."

"It's a deal."

"What happens to Chet if he doesn't accept this
deal?"

Shana tried to make herself more comfortable in
her chair. "Not stated."

"What's inferred?"

"Chet worries he'll be cut off. Find himself on
some South Pacific island selling pocket mirrors."

"Nonsense. He must have his own abilities."

"You know what I mean."

"No, I don't know what you mean."

"It's all or nothing. If Chet wants the benefits of
being Chester Radliegh's son, which benefits are
considerable, he has to conform to a pattern of be-
havior, at least image, which permits him to accomplish all that Chester Radliegh's son can. That's
reasonable, isn't it?"

"Do you have any idea how Chet himself feels
about this?"

Beautiful in her yellow bikini in her cushioned
white rattan chair, Shana looked uncomfortable.
"Rage." She cleared her throat.

"What?"

"Rage. He's enraged. He's got his nose right up
against a brick wall. His father pushed him into

sports, football in particular. Chet found himself
building this hunk body. Became All-American. His
father pushed him academically. Chet became Phi
Beta Kappa. History. His father pushed him
through Law School. You see, Chester had this
plan for him all along. Chet always knew he was
gay. He was straight with his father about it. When
Chet discovered his father had had this book written for him, he was furious. Hurt. When he discovered his father had established what you might
call a retirement plan for the local incumbent congressman, he was even more furious. He flunked
the Bar Exam. I believe he flunked it on purpose.
Chet had never failed at anything in his life. He
knows for a certainty that whatever he does he cannot satisfy his father. Being gay doesn't worry Chet
at all. It's that he can't satisfy his father no matter
what he does. He can't get away from his father's
'arrangements' unless he gets entirely away, gives
up everything. Do you see?"

"I guess."

"Do you have a, you know what I mean, father,
Jack?"

"Yes."

"Does any of this seem familiar to you?"

Jack shook his head. "He's never been a problem
to me. Not enough of a one."

"That's nice."

"Unusual, I guess. I mean . . . I don't know what
I mean."

"Fathers are confusing."

"I guess."

"I told you about my father."

"Yes."

"A cheap, undisciplined weasel of a man who gladly rapes truth for a Mercedes-Benz."

"So it was Doctor Radliegh who chose you to be Chet's wife."

"Yes. He brought me here last spring on the pretext of business and told Chet that he, Chet, is to marry me."

"How did Chet react to that?"

"He gets to keep his ... whatever. His stable-boys."

"Shana?" Jack asked. "Are you and Doctor Radliegh lovers?"

"Yes," Shana answered.

"I see. Are you real lovers?"

"Oh, yes. Chester doesn't play around."

"Oh."

"We have been for over a year. Since we found ourselves alone one weekend in Berlin. Neither one of us planned it, expected it. I didn't. To me, Chester was Big Boss, as formal as a royal reception. It was unimaginable to me he would ever react, relate to me, in any way, except as courteous boss. There was a snowstorm. Some business people didn't show up for dinner. We found ourselves having dinner together. Laughing. Then throwing snowballs at each other in the street. Then licking the snow off each other's faces. Then in bed together. Have you met Mrs. Radliegh?"

"Briefly."

"She can't stand success. She thought she was marrying a college instructor. She found herself some kind of an Empress. It depressed her totally. Some people can't stand changes. Her misery depressed him totally. She works at it. She made him miserable. Chester could never bring himself to divorcing the poor mess. I understand that. Well, her misery depresses him less now."

"Since you two got together."

"Since he discovered it's her nature and there is nothing he can do about it." Then she said, "Yes. Since we got together."

"Does Chet know you and his father are lovers?"

"No. He thinks I'm marrying him for money. Social position."

"Shana, you've been frank about everything else. Are you doing this for money, social position?"

"I really love Chester."

She seemed more comfortable in her chair.

"I believe you do."

"I love him deeply. I never dreamed of knowing, loving such a man. I never could have conceived such a man existed. Or that such a man would need me, love me."

"I'm beginning to get the picture," Jack said. "Chet in Washington. You here at Vindemia."

"Sounds nice to me."

"Would you have children by Chester?"

"We've talked about it. I would like to."

"Surely then Chet would know you and his father are lovers."

Shana smiled. "I expect there would be a proper family resemblance among the children."

"Um," Jack said. "I can't think what could go wrong in such a marriage."

She smiled. "Convenient."

"As you said: very convenient."

"So," Shana said. "You know about Chet. And me. And Chester. What a good little investigative reporter you are. What else do you know? Who is threatening Chester?"

"Now I see the level of your concern."

"I think I'm the only one who is concerned about him."

"You may be. You and Mrs. Houston."

"She's a good old thing."

There was the sound of children in the air.

"It's pretty sad," Jack said. "Mrs. Radliegh must be half crazed with drink and drugs."

"Eccentric," Shana said.

"Duncan seems to have a taste for drugs of another kind."

"Is that what's wrong with him? I thought he was just a dumb slob."

"That, too. He lies. He cheats. He wants $650,000 for a new car."

"Let him ride a bike."

"Alixis thinks she would like life better without her father interfering."

"Without her father, Alixis would be standing on

a street corner in white boots and a leather mini-skirt."

"Beauville—"

"We're being invaded," Shana said.

A boy about nine years old, naked except for water wings, entered the pool area. Big-eyed, he stared across at them.

"Chester the Third," Shana said. "Except I forget his last name. Among them, Amy's seven children have three different last names."

Jack said, "I guess we're not supposed to be caught in social intercourse, you and I. But none of the other rules around here seem to be unbroken."

Shana said, "Rules ought not be broken."

One by one four more children tottered into the pool area. Except for water wings they were all naked. Their bodies were entirely tanned. Their bodies all had good shape to them, less baby fat and more muscle than usual for such young children.

A gaunt woman carrying a two year old entered the pool area. She was followed by a uniformed nanny carrying an infant.

Jack stood up. "I guess I had better go."

"Me, too."

"Where are you going?" Jack asked. "What are you going to do now?"

"Why?"

"Just curious. I wonder what you do around here, how you spend your time. I wonder what Vindemia means to you."

"I'm going to the gym to work out."

"So you can mention to Doctor Radliegh that you did?"

"Because I want to."

Jack crossed to the wading pool. The gaunt woman was setting the two year old into the water.

"I don't know your name," he said to the gaunt woman.

"Amy MacDowell is the short version."

"Well, I guess I should leave," Jack said to her. "Now that you're all here."

"I wish you wouldn't." She waved good bye to Shana as she left the pool. "We could use an extra pair of eyes. Lifeguard."

"Oh. Okay."

Jack returned to his chair in the shade. Happily the children were jumping off the edge of the pool to splash each other. They did not lack for energy.

Amy carried the infant into the shade. She sat in the chair near Jack where Shana had sat.

She began to suckle the infant.

"You didn't tell me your name," she said.

"Jack."

She pointed to one of the boys. "His name is Jack. John. Named after his father."

Of the seven children, four were boys.

"These are all your children?"

"Yes. Aren't they beautiful?"

"Yes."

"I do this really well."

"What?"

"Have children. It took three husbands, so far, but each one of them was handsome, healthy, and bright enough."

"You're not yet thirty?"

"Twenty nine."

"Wow. Seven children while you're under thirty. Pardon me. I just haven't met that before."

She laughed.

"And you want more children?" he asked.

"Yes. Lots."

"Good thing you're rich."

"Yes. Isn't that nice? Has anyone ever told you what a pleasure it is to nurse a baby?"

"It looks nice."

"Envious of little Robert here?"

"I guess so."

"Were you nursed?"

"I have no idea."

"Then I suspect you weren't. I believe nursed babies are much better off."

"Your husbands—? Never mind."

She laughed. "Well, in order to have all these children, you see, really I'm better off living here at Vindemia, where there is plenty of help. The men I've married think they would be happy living here. But, in time, they discover they're not a bit happy. Each has found Vindemia much too confining."

"I can understand that."

"And here they either work for my father, or they don't work. There isn't anything else to do.

Slowly they get restless, and finally, you know, make the speech of apology, say they can't take it anymore, they have to go live their own lives. We're all good friends, I and my ex-husbands, that is. I understand."

"You wanted these kids pretty badly, didn't you?"

"Oh, yes. Don't you think having lots of nice children is a good use of wealth?"

Jack said, "I've seen worse uses."

Politely, conversationally, Amy then asked Jack personal questions, where he had been born, brought up, schooled. He answered as well as he could.

She said, "You're old enough to be married. You never were?"

"No."

"I expect you have a fairly hopeless view of marriage."

"Except to have children, maybe . . ."

"Don't you want children?"

"I don't know."

"Sure," she said. "It's the only reason to get married. Just to keep the paperwork straight."

Jack said, "Shedding yourself of three husbands must have cost more than a little."

"Oh, that," she said. "I have a way of handling my father."

"How's that?" he asked.

"If he doesn't do what I want I'll tell the world he sexually abused me as a child."

"Is it true?"

"Of course not. But he manipulates, tries to control everybody. One has to have a way of manipulating him, don't you agree? His reputation, that he's Mister Perfect himself, perfect husband, father of a perfect family, is his soft spot. It's the only weapon I have, you see."

"It's not very nice."

"It works."

"Would you actually use it? Say such a thing?"

"Of course. And he knows it."

The oldest boy, about nine years old, was standing between Jack's knees. "What's your name?" he asked.

"Jack."

"Jack, will you come play with us?"

Jack wasn't sure he wanted to play with the children in the pool.

He was sure he wanted no more of the conversation with Amy MacDowell.

Suddenly the beautiful day, the beautiful flowers, the beautiful pool, the beautiful children seemed to have become splattered by something foul.

"Go ahead," Amy said.

Jack stood up. "If I touch your naked children in the swimming pool will I be accused of sexual child abuse?" His voice sounded stronger to him than he had intended.

"Of course not." Amy chuckled. "What would be the point?"

Jack enjoyed himself more than he thought.

Cupping his hands under water, one by one the children stepped into his hands so he could lift them out of the water and fling them backward. They landed on their backs, laughing, making lovely splashes.

The children then began a game of King of the Mountain with him, each trying to climb him, sit on his shoulders, throw the others off. His hair got pulled and his ears tugged.

The children wriggled around with the energy and humor of monkeys.

The games continued longer than he expected.

"Jack?" Amy called him from the side of the pool. "You'd better come out of the water, now. Your back is bleeding."

Jack put his own hand on his back and saw it was so.

"Besides," Amy said. "The sun will scar your cut."

While Jack was putting on his socks and sneakers, Amy said to him, "Don't tell anybody what I told you. I'd hate to have Alixis use it against my father, too. You know what I mean?"

17

"**Y**ou make sweet sounds come out of that stringed box."

Jack was sitting in the woods, his back against a tree, strumming his guitar. His bike was propped against another tree.

First a boxer dog had bounded into the little clearing in the woods; then a tall, lean older man wearing walking shorts and horned-rimmed glasses came along the path. The man had a long, very straight back.

"Don't get up," Doctor Radliegh said. "And don't stop playing. I like it. May I sit down, Jack?"

Jack resettled his back against the tree. "They're your woods, Doctor Radliegh."

"God's woods. God's world. We're just the caretakers." Radliegh sat cross-legged on a tuft of grass. He chuckled. "If I were God, I'd fire us. Wouldn't you?"

"If you were God, would you fire you?" Jack asked.

"I've tried to keep my patch neat." Radliegh looked around at the planted forest. "Make the most of it. How does one play a guitar?"

"I've been doing it so long . . ." Jack did a short riff. "Just let your fingers play, I guess."

After a lunch of sandwiches and milk in his cottage, Jack had strapped the guitar on his back and gone for a bike ride around Vindemia.

There were only a few cars outside the business offices on Saturday afternoon. Beauville's BMW was one.

There were more than a dozen small airplanes, both jets and propeller driven, parked neatly on the airstrip. As Jack watched, an ancient yellow two-seater wobbled down the sky and made a perfect landing. There seemed to be only one person, the pilot, a man, in it.

Again, there were only a few cars outside the country club. The tennis courts, pool area, and greens were devoid of people.

While heading toward the airstrip, a gray Infiniti sedan with tinted windows passed Jack. Another passed him from behind before he went on the road around the country club.

Jack presumed guests were arriving in the airplanes and then being ferried to the main house for the party that night.

Beyond the clubhouse, Jack found a timber road heading off to the right. Intersecting with it were walking-riding trails. He jounced his bike along one until he came to a clearing where he thought he'd be alone.

He had been playing his guitar for only about twenty minutes.

Another plane went overhead, low.

Doctor Chester Radliegh looked up through the trees from where he sat cross-legged on the ground. "Lots of guests arriving." He smiled at Jack. "Good time to take a walk."

"You know my name," Jack said.

Radliegh nodded. "Jack Faoni."

The dog climbed onto Radliegh's crossed legs and lay down on them. His settled his chin on Radliegh's knee.

Radliegh said, "This guy's name is Arky. He thinks I belong to him."

"Arky?"

"Archimedes."

"Of course."

"Wanted to name a son that, but Mrs. Radliegh would have none of it."

"Name a son after a screw?" Jack smiled.

"Never mind." Conversationally, Radliegh said, "A few days ago my elder son, Chet, surprised me. He met me at the stables at dawn. He had saddled two horses. We had a great ride together."

Jack waited for the point of this comment.

Radliegh said no more.

Jack asked, "Where was Peppy that morning?"

"I don't know."

Searching for a point, Jack asked, "How many days was this before your favorite horse died?"

"Oh, days," Radliegh answered. "Three or four days." He patted the dog's head. "Things like that don't happen as often as I expected they would."

"Like what?" Jack asked.

"Oh, just one of the kids joining me for a ride."

Thinking about Radliegh, Jack played a short, fast ditty on the guitar.

Jack was thinking he had never before met a mind like Radliegh's. The man was a certified genius, but there was something childlike in what Radliegh had just said. Or was it subtle, profound?

Radliegh was surprised his children did not join him for rides.

Radliegh was surprised one son, one day, did join him for a ride.

Therefore . . . what?

When Jack had asked Nancy Dunbar why the need for all the security and spying at Vindemia, she had said: "Doctor Radliegh does not like surprises."

Perhaps Radliegh's mind was on a plane so different from the average person's that everything about humans surprised him.

Intensely, Radliegh had watched Jack's fingers play the ditty. "That's fun," he said.

"So how does one invent the perfect mirror?" Jack asked.

Radliegh shrugged. "Just like your fingers. Let your mind play; pick at things: something develops." Then he said, "Sometimes."

Looking at his fingers on the frets, Jack asked, "What happens to a black hole when it disappears?"

Radliegh smiled. "You mean, what happens to the information within?"

"I don't know what I mean."

"It would be fun if it elongated into a line so narrow that its cut length would be a speck so small it might be invisible."

"Why would that be fun?" Jack asked.

"Because it might help define the indefinite we're prone to think of as the infinite."

"Oh." Jack did not understand, but he heard the readiness to answer, the words. Doctor Radliegh may be surprised by humans, perhaps had inadequate language to deal with them, but he was not surprised black holes appeared to disappear.

"Do you mind my asking what your mind is playing with, picking at now?" Jack asked.

"Of course not," Radliegh said. "Space locomotion."

"Space travel?"

"I guess so. I don't believe people are questioning sufficiently the basic principles of physics."

Jack said, "I'm not."

"You were taught not."

"Only thing we were taught to question," Jack said, "was our marks, not our teachers."

"That is," Radliegh continued rapidly, "that the basic laws of physics are universal, cosmological.

Considering the history of the cosmos, we humans have been perceiving physical laws as briefly as it takes you to blink your eye, comparatively."

Jack blinked.

"I'm not sure sufficient weight is given to the fact that our perceptions, so far considered absolute, are entirely dependent upon our intellectual appurtenances. These physical laws, seen from another planet, dependent upon other intellectual appurtenances, might be perceived entirely differently. Probably are."

"Okay."

"Yet the true, absolute, ultimate physical laws might conform to no perception of them yet achieved on any planet, be totally different."

Jack said, "I guess I'll stick to pickin' my guitar."

"It's the same thing," Radliegh said. "Your achieving a system of time and space permits you to play the guitar. We have to achieve a system of time and space presently inconceivable to us to achieve space travel."

Radliegh lifted the boxer dog off his legs and stood it on its own legs on the ground. "Well, come on, Arky." Radliegh stood. "Guess I've got to go be polite." Standing up, Radliegh said, "You see, it's okay to think about anything, however silly. That's how questions develop."

Feet spread, hands over his head, Doctor Radliegh stretched fully. "It's a silly thought, of course, totally without basis, but wouldn't it be nice if, for example, the elongated black holes had the information to be tramways, to get us through space quickly?"

From where Jack sat on the ground the stretching man seemed huge.

"One suggestion, or hope, always is," Radliegh continued, as he crouched and petted Arky, "that everything has a purpose. Not to look for the purpose, not to see it, to see it and deny it, is fault, wouldn't you say?"

"Sir?" Jack asked.

Smiling, Radliegh waited for Jack to speak.

"How come you sat and talked with me?" Jack asked. "Said such things to me? I mean, from your own mind?"

Radliegh's eyebrows shot up. "My way of saying thank you," he said, "for your concern. Someday you might have the kindness to remember I did so."

Which left Jack totally, absolutely confused.

Jack wondered if he was seeing Chester Radliegh from the right planet.

18

In his blue bow tie, carrying his silver tray, at dusk Jack approached a group of formally dressed people on one of the terraces of the main house at Vindemia.

"Would you care for an hors d'oeuvre, sir?"

Turning around suddenly, a man grabbed the silver tray firmly with his left hand and held it steady. "Ah! Liver wrapped in bacon! One of my favorite things!"

Jack said, "D—!"

"You almost dropped the tray, lad!" Fletch said, letting it go. "Want to see us all dressed so pretty at a grand party at Vindemia on our hands and knees eating liver wrapped in bacon off the terrace floor? That would be a pretty sight!"

The two women to whom Fletch had been talking tittered.

Then Fletch thrust his face close to Jack's and whispered, "Can you spell it?"

His eyes on them, Doctor Chester Radliegh guided his wife across the terrace to Fletch.

"What?"

"Hors d'oeuvre."

"Sure."

"Good! Your grandmother never could."

"My grandmother? The mystery novelist?"

"Your grandmother, the defective novelist," Fletch said.

"Mister Fletcher!" Radliegh held out his hand to Fletch. "I'm Chester Radliegh."

"How nice of you to have me on such short notice!" Fletch took Radliegh's hand.

"I've wanted to meet you for a long time," Radliegh said. "I'm a great fan of your biography of Edgar Arthur Tharpe Junior."

Glaring at Jack, Fletch sniffed. "Some like it."

"My wife," Radliegh introduced, "Amalie."

"So pleased to meet you, Doctor Fletcher."

"No doctor at all," Fletch said. "Not even a patient. Call me Irwin."

"Irwin?" Jack muttered. "Since when Irwin?"

"Where are you from originally?" Amalie asked. Her eyes were glazed with complete indifference.

Jack noticed that, unlike her appearance that morning, not one hair on Amalie Radliegh's head was either out of place or gray. Although still puffy, the skin of her face was smooth and had good color.

"Montana," Fletch answered.

"Montana!" Jack expostulated behind Fletch's back. "Since when Montana?"

"Mister Fletcher," Radliegh said, "I thought I wouldn't show you the Bierstadt until morning. It's in the gym. The light will be better in the morning."

"That's fine," Fletch said.

Behind Fletch's back, Jack whispered, "What's a Bierstadt?"

"Although I will say hanging a precious painting in a gymnasium strikes me as odd."

"Oh," Jack said. "A painting."

"You haven't seen the gym." Radliegh smiled. "The painting is perfectly safe there. Temperature and humidity controlled. Its size and power, vigor seem well suited to the gym."

Amalie said, "My husband is eccentric."

Then she said to Fletch: "And tell me: do you speak coyote?"

Each entertaining a separate group around the terrace were Chet, Amy, Downes, Beauville, Nancy Dunbar. Neither Alixis nor Duncan was there.

"I wonder if after dinner you might join me in the study," Radliegh asked Fletch. "I figure it will be my only chance to have a quiet chat with you about your book, *Pinto*. Reading your biography sometime ago, I made notes, never thinking I'd have the opportunity to meet you."

"Of course," Fletch said. "That will be fine."

"Ten o'clock then," Radliegh said.

Fletch said, "See you."

As the Radlieghs drew off, Fletch turned to Jack.

"Get rid of the tray, will you? We need a walk and talk."

"How did you get here?" Jack asked.

"Radliegh has a painting he wants to sell. I can't afford it, of course, but he doesn't know that."

Jack handed his tray of hors d'oeuvres to Peppy, who already had one. Now he had a tray in each hand.

"Here," Fletch said to Peppy. "I'll help you." He picked an hors d'oeuvre off one of the trays.

"Thanks a lot," Peppy said. "Sir."

"Any time."

Fletch and Jack walked down the terrace steps.

"I'll show you my digs," Jack said.

Fletch said, "I suppose I can be late, but I really ought to be back in time for the dinner." They were walking around the lit pool. A few young from the party idled in the pool area. They glanced at the white-jacketed man in black tie walking into the gardens with a young waiter. "Tell me everything you know."

Jack said, "That would take forever."

"I haven't got forever."

As they walked the bricked paths through the indirectly lit landscaped gardens, Jack said, "There are more rules for living here than there are in a military academy. Or a monastery. And they are all circumvented, seemingly by everybody."

"Things are a little oppressive at Vindemia, is that it? The cork is kept on pretty tight?"

"To the point of rebellion," Jack said. "I've

heard even the C.E.O., Eric Beauville, say he feels a prisoner here."

"Talk to me," Fletch said.

"The rebellion isn't open," Jack said. "Everyone just sneaks around spending more energy circumventing the rules than they seem to spend doing anything positive. Like living. Working. So there's a kind of gridlock."

Enjoying the flora and fauna of the garden paths, Fletch said, "Gridlock in paradise. Could it be otherwise? I've always suspected Adam and Eve sinned out of pure boredom."

Jack described how the Chief Executive Officer, Eric Beauville, and Radliegh's private secretary, Nancy Dunbar, hide their smoking cigarettes; everyone from Radliegh's wife to his stableboy hide their liquor; daughter Alixis her wild sex compulsions; son Duncan his lying, cheating and use of hard drugs.

"Busy little place," Fletch said, "for all that."

Jack said, "Radliegh knows his son, Chet, is gay."

" 'Gay,' " Fletch repeated.

"Chet doesn't respond to girls at all. Peppy, that kid you just so thoughtfully helped by making one of his trays lighter, is the stableboy and Chet's lover."

"But Shana—?"

"Is Doctor Radliegh's lover."

"Ah, ha! Doing double duty as Chet's fiancée to keep up the image necessary for Chet's impending national political career."

"You know a few things yourself."

"Thanks to Andy Cyst. I thought you said there's no story here."

Jack said, "Not one to tell."

"No," Fletch said. "Not one to tell."

"Come in." Jack opened the door to his half of the cottage.

"There's no lock on your door," Fletch said.

"I've noticed."

"I guess when you've got a chain-link fence around the whole estate, only one gate, guards at it, not every door within the estate needs to be locked."

"We're protected from everything but our protectors," Jack said. "We even have passports we have to show to enter the estate."

"Passports?"

"Even have to show them at the company store to buy food. Mine's pink."

Fletch glanced around the small living-dining room, kitchenette. "Do you suppose this place is bugged?"

"Do I care?"

"Ah," Fletch said. "Doesn't take you long to get rebellious. I must remember that next time you visit and I ask you to take a shower."

Jack said, "There was a murder here. I think that much is pretty clear. In a laboratory which was not supposed to have lethal gas in it, Doctor Jim Wilson was killed by lethal gas. He wasn't supposed to be in the laboratory at that moment. Radliegh was."

"Is the death being investigated?"

"It must be. Unnatural death, all that. But I've seen no sign of it."

"Radliegh can't keep the police out."

"I haven't seen any police around—other than his own rent-a-cops."

Wandering around the room, Jack then talked generally of almost everything he had seen, heard, thought, felt since arriving at Vindemia.

"Okay, Jack. You've been here a while." Fletch relaxed in the two-seater couch. "Who's making all these attempts on Chester Radliegh's life?"

"Process of elimination?" Jack asked. "Motive? Opportunity?"

"Any method at your command."

"Well, his mother-in-law isn't. She's a strong old dear, and the only one around here who seems genuinely appreciative, respectful of Doctor Radliegh. She seems to think he really is perfect."

"Pretty old, is she? All her illicit compulsions behind her?"

"I doubt Mrs. Radliegh could organize these attempts. You just met her. Amalie."

"Do you suppose she really thinks coyote is a language? Or was she trying to tell me she's nuts?"

"Her brain is filled with little pills bumping into each other in a pool of liquor."

Fletch said, "She could have fixed the coffeepot to electrocute her husband."

"Yes, she could have," Jack agreed. "That wouldn't have taken much doing. It was in his personal dressing room. But the cabin explosion, the broken front axle on the Jeep—"

"I've been thinking about that," Fletch said. "Sounds to me like the work of two different people, working at cross-purposes. Radliegh didn't get blown up in the cabin because the Jeep axle broke first. Also possibly true in what happened in the laboratory. One person filled it with poison gas; another arranged a bomb in the building. You were right. Too much time went by between Wilson's being poisoned by gas and the explosion."

"Daughter Amy is the only one who seems to have her father where she wants him. She's told him if she doesn't get what she wants, she'll falsely accuse him of sexually abusing her as a child."

"Nice."

"It seems to be working. So she has no motive for knocking off her father. She has seven children she keeps here, and, has gotten Papa to pay off three husbands."

"What some women will do to protect themselves from controlling men. In olden times, some became witches, for the same reason. Later, others bought bikes and got jobs."

"He's got more reason to kill her, than she him, to my mind. And Peppy says anybody could have poisoned the horse—if the horse was poisoned."

"Poison is easy to get, especially on a farm. Any

kind of poison could have been used, from a stim-
ulant to a depressant."

"Well, Mrs. Radliegh uses depressants. And
stimulants, I guess. I emptied her rubbish this
morning. But I don't see her tiptoeing around a
stable before dawn."

"Lethal gas is something else. I would think that
could be traced. It had to come from somewhere."

"So," Jack said. "It looks to me more than one
person is making attempts on Radliegh's life."

"Me, too." Fletch stood up. "You've eliminated
very few people, if any. And that leaves a lot of
suspects. Rather too many." He patted his cum-
berbund. "A few days with your mother has made
me uncommonly hungry."

"She has that effect," Jack said. "Did you enjoy
your time with her at all?"

"Definitely I did. Your mother's wise and witty,"
Fletch said. "Always has been. I suppose at some
point during the last twenty years I could have
looked her up. Should have."

"Do you feel badly about not having done so?"

Fletch looked at his son in the lamplight of the
small room. "I do now."

"You had no real reason to," Jack said. "You
didn't know about me. She didn't tell you. In fact,
she was sort of hiding from you."

"That's not nice to think about."

"And, people do drop from sight."

"The question now is," Fletch said, "what are

we going to do about Radliegh? You called me here—"

"Thanks for coming, by the way."

"I want to see that Bierstadt anyway. There appear to have been a number of attempts on his life; one succeeded in killing an innocent bystander. The methods of trying to kill him have been distinctly different, even maybe contradictory."

"Lots of attempts," Jack said. "Lots of suspects."

"Different methods, from poisons to bombs. And one successful murderer. And, I don't see that Chester Radliegh deserves being murdered in particular, do you?"

"He sat with me in a patch of woods this afternoon," Jack said, "and talked to me. You sort of feel like you're sitting next to a nuclear-powered aircraft carrier, or something, but other than that, he's a nice guy."

"I mean, he hasn't committed mass murder, raped his daughter, drugged his wife and son, ground the faces of the poor . . ."

"If anything, to the contrary."

"Well." Fletch glanced at his watch. "I'm meeting with Radliegh at ten o'clock."

Jack said, "Maybe it's that no one talks to him. I mean, really talks to him. It seemed to me this afternoon that, for him, people are a long reach, if you know what I mean."

"You know, Jack," Fletch said at the door. "Even King George the Third got the point, after a while."

19

"Listen, dear lady," Mortimer lectured gently. He sat by Crystal's bed. "We have only two real sources of energy. One is sleep. The other is food."

The telephone he had placed in the corner of the gymnasium for Crystal's use rang.

"You must not spend all night every night reading. Man does not live by literature alone. You need sleep."

"I get hungry. Too hungry to sleep," Crystal said. "I mean, I used to think I was hungry."

"That's the good dear. You're beginning to understand."

Mortimer answered the phone. "Hello? Oh, my God, it's that Fletcher bird. I thought we got rid of you, Fletcher. Please at least tell me you've left the state of Wyoming?"

"I've left the state," Fletch said.

"That's the best thing I've heard about Wyoming since I've been here—you've left."

Talking on his personal communicator, Fletch was walking back through the twisting, landscaped walks to Vindemia's main house. "Just want to know how you two are getting along."

"Better without you," Mortimer said.

"Either one of you killed the other yet?"

"I am enjoying Crystal's company enormously."

"You are?"

"Best company I've had in years. What a charming lady! She tells wonderful stories."

"Yeah. I know."

"Nothing about the boxing world, of course. Those stories I tell," Mortimer said. "To her, they're news."

"So you're grateful I brought Crystal to you?"

"And then left."

"I didn't feel all that welcome this morning."

"You weren't."

"I mean, we weren't as well received at your place as we might have been. Under the circumstances."

"Better than you deserved. We didn't shoot you. Well, we did shoot at you, but we didn't succeed in killing you, more's the pity."

"You couldn't have hit me from more than arm's length away even if you had succeeded in reloading the gun."

"I seem to remember you on the ground, on your back."

"I tripped."

"That's what Schmeling said."

"What happened to gratitude?"

"It came in last in the last race at Hialeah. Hasn't been heard from since."

"Okay, I give up," Fletch said. "Is Crystal within reach of the phone? I want to make sure she's still among the living and breathing."

"Here," Mortimer said. "She lives. She breathes. With a friend like you, I don't know why she bothers."

"Fletch?" Crystal asked. "Where are you?"

"Vindemia."

"How could you be? That's in Georgia. You left here just this morning."

"I was propelled by Mister Mortimer's bad breath."

"Have you seen Jack?"

"Just left him. He's fine. How are you?"

"Having a wonderful time! Whatever convinced you Mister Mortimer is the solution to my problems?"

"At frequent great risk to myself, I am determined to see the best in people."

"I'm even exercising!"

"How's that?"

"He strapped wrist weights and ankle weights on me. I've been doing arm lifts and leg lifts in bed."

"Lifting weights in bed? I've done that."

"Earlier I did five sit-ups. Later three sit-ups. I'm scheduled to do one more. I feel the blood coursing through my veins vigorously."

"You must be exhausted."

"He gives me frequent high-energy snacks. The food makes me want to do these exercises. 'Shrinking the belly,' he calls it."

In Vindemia's dark gardens, Fletch envisioned Crystal's mammoth white belly shrinking. Then he envisioned the polar ice cap melting. "That's good."

"Watching the boys here in the gym inspires me. My God, the energy they spend. They jump rope, lift weights for hours, it seems, beat up punching bags, beat up each other, then do one-armed chinups just for fun. I didn't know even boys could have so much energy!"

Fletch said, "It's why war was invented."

"I think I inspire them, too. Every once in a while they look over at me, the great burial mound—and throw themselves back into their training, speed up. Well, seeing what all they do makes me lift my arms and legs a few more times. We drive each other on."

"Mister Mortimer is being nice enough?"

"He's a dear. Such a gentleman!"

"Poo," Fletch said. "If he's a gentleman, I'm a trout."

"You're a trout. He couldn't be more considerate, charming, encouraging. He says I'll be doing standing exercises within five days, beginning to hike within seven."

"Just don't wreck the punching bags, Crystal. I mean, it actually is possible to hit them too hard."

"I'm not to think about losing weight. It will just happen."

"That sounds right."

"My goal is not to lose weight; it's to change my way of life, my way of thinking."

"Your perceptions of yourself."

"How's Carrie? Did you see her?"

"I stopped by the farm this afternoon to get a change of clothes. She's well. She's waiting for a mare to drop her filly."

"Why would a Mayor drop cream cheese?"

"Crystal, you're still thinking food."

"Fletch, did you happen to notice the younger boy here?"

"Ricky? Yes."

"There's something about him."

"Something . . . What?"

"I don't know. Standing still, being quiet, still he oozes some kind of power."

"Sex?"

"More than that." Crystal separated her words with pauses. "One cannot help listening to him, watching him."

"Is he handsome, attractive, what?"

"It's something else . . ."

"Charisma?"

"I read to him this afternoon, from a book that just happened to be here, Steinbeck's *Of Mice and Men*."

"Mister Mortimer reads Steinbeck?"

"He has lots of books."

"He does?"

"At first, I was just reading to Ricky. He was sitting by my bed. Then I began to feel things from him."

"From Steinbeck? Of course."

"No. From Ricky. Then I started watching him as I read. He was hardly moving. His legs were twisted around each other. I couldn't actually see the muscles of his shoulders, chest, arms, hands, even his face moving, but they were moving. I could feel them moving. I couldn't hear or see him breathing, but I could tell his breathing was under some kind of intense control. His eyes were pulsing. Is that the right word?"

"I don't know."

"What I mean is that he was so into it . . . he was feeling it, every word . . . he was reacting physically to it . . . but I couldn't see exactly what he was doing, or how he was doing it."

"In other words, even while you were reading Steinbeck, somehow Ricky was making you watch him."

"Yeah. Something like that. Can you explain it?"

"No. Yes."

"Mister Mortimer here is making faces at me." Fletch heard a grumble from the background. "He says, 'Damned kid looked so much at himself in a mirror he fell into it and now he wants everybody else to join him there.' " Crystal laughed.

"Mister Mortimer said that?"

"What's your explanation?"

"No explanation. Just a question."

"What's the question?"

"With which are you in love, Crystal? Mister Mortimer? Or Ricky? Or both?"

"You think I'm in love? Maybe. I love Wyoming. Oops, that did it! Mister Mortimer says I have to hang up now. It's time for my sit-up."

Fletch had waited on a high spot at the edge of the gardens until he had finished his conversation with Crystal.

At almost eye level was the large terrace of Vindemia's main house. Men in white jackets and bow ties, women in their pretty summer dresses milled around.

At the side of the terrace opposite the bar and serving tables a string quartet played Haydn.

With his straight back, light glinting from his horn-rimmed glasses, Doctor Chester Radliegh was urging his guests in to dinner.

Fletch noticed that variously colored lights, party lights, were built into the walls of the house facing the terrace, as well as the low walls surrounding it. Simply by switching them on, these lights would give the terrace a party glow even if no one were there partying.

For a moment Fletch watched the rich, brilliant man, gracious and graceful host, smiling, inviting his many friends into his home for dinner.

The rich, brilliant, gracious and graceful man whom more than one person was trying to murder.

Slipping the little telephone into his jacket's pocket, Fletch rejoined the party.

20

"**C**lose the door."

Doctor Chester Radliegh was standing at an angle between a highly polished mahogany desk and mahogany floor-to-ceiling bookshelves in his study at Vindemia. Directly in front of him in its own mahogany stand was a world globe.

It was ten o'clock.

Fletch closed the door.

"Would you like a cognac?" Radliegh asked.

Approaching, Fletch said, "You drink cognac?"

"On occasion."

"Sure."

On a shelf at the base of the window separating the bookshelves behind his desk, Radliegh poured cognac into two snifters on a silver tray.

Nowhere on the desk, nowhere visible in the room was a copy of Fletch's book, *Pinto*.

Fletch took the snifter. "Thank you."

"Mister Fletcher," Radliegh said as he inhaled

from his snifter, "I want to thank you and your son for showing your concern for me—well, for another human being—by coming here to help solve what you see as my problems."

"My son?"

"Yes. The pool boy. Jack Faoni. The young man who was serving hors d'oeuvres on the terrace before dinner."

"You know he's my son?"

"You two circling each other on the terrace whispering questions and answers, making jokes, I believe, behind each other's backs only each other could hear, and, I daresay, appreciate, was a piece of theater I would have regretted missing."

Jack had said something to Fletch about being next to Chester Radliegh was like being next to a nuclear powered aircraft carrier: overwhelming.

Fletch said, "You can't possibly know Jack Faoni is my son. Even your lover, Shana Staufel, doesn't know it."

Radliegh smiled. "People here at Vindemia believe all the phones are tapped, and that the one outside the General Store is not."

Fletch said, "And that's the one that is."

Radliegh said, "It's much cheaper, more efficient to tap one phone than dozens. Surely you can see that."

"Yes," Fletch said. "I can see that." Radliegh knew every word Jack had said to him while Fletch was driving into Wyoming. "Did you invite me here so I can sing 'Git Along Little Dogies' to you?"

"I invited you here to thank you. And to assure you that everything is fine."

"Everything is not fine," Fletch said.

"And, by now, I assume you and your son have had a long chat and he has filled you in on everything he has learned about me and my household."

"Right again."

"Shana called Jack in without my knowledge or permission. I was very surprised to read the notes of her conversation with him from the phone outside—"

"—the General Store."

"Reading those notes, something about Shana was confirmed, and, I learned something else about her. What was confirmed was her very real love, passion, and concern for me. What I learned is that snow turns her on in a way I hadn't realized."

"Beg pardon?"

"Apparently, a few years ago, she grabbed your sweating son in the snow in Stowe, Vermont, one night, tore his shirt off him, and hustled him to her bed for a few hours of passionate love crawl."

"Oh."

"You didn't know that?"

"He hasn't told me that part, yet."

"It was in Berlin on a night snow was falling a year ago Shana and I discovered ourselves having a snowball fight in the street, shoving fresh snow down each other's collars, etc." Radliegh's smile was shy. "Also confirmed was that there was nothing contrived about Shana and me ending up in bed together that night. Not that I thought there was. As a result of this discovery, I am making arrangements for business conferences in St. Moritz this next winter."

"Shana really loves you," Fletch posited. "Is that what you're saying?"

"Passionately. Isn't that nice?"

"Wonderful."

"So she called Jack. Jack came here. And he called you. And you came here. By the way, I did read *Pinto*, and enjoyed it."

"No notes?"

"Of course notes. No questions, though. None that I remember."

"That's good. I felt I was facing an oral examination tonight."

"No examination at all," Radliegh said. "Just a simple thank you, and a statement that there is no problem."

"There is a problem."

"Are you genuinely interested in the Bierstadt?"

"I'd like to see it."

"Fine. I'll show it to you in the morning, as planned, before you leave."

"Doctor Radliegh, someone, more than one is, I mean, are trying to kill you."

"So what?" Radliegh's fingers rubbed his chest. "So what?"

"How many attempts on my life do you and Jack,

and Shana, count? Four?"

"The coffeepot, the exploded cabin, the broken axle on the Jeep, the possibly poisoned horse—"

"Try eighteen. That's a good number. Try twenty-four."

"These attempts have been going on that long?"

"I don't know much about your education, Mister Fletcher, but somewhere along the way you must have picked up some scientific method." Radliegh raised his left arm over his head and flexed it. "When you see four or five attempts on my life, you are right to be alarmed. When you've seen two dozen or so the proof, if you will, is that none has succeeded."

"One did succeed. And I don't think Doctor Jim Wilson was thinking primarily of scientific method while he was dying of lethal gas poisoning meant for you in your laboratory."

"I trust he was. And whom do you accuse? My wife? You know Shana Staufel and I are lovers."

"I sat beside your wife at dinner," Fletch said. There had been sixty at dinner, and Fletch had been put at the foot of the table. "She kept talking about what she called 'upsetting passions,' even asking me to name mine. She seems to feel everyone around her is driven by one passion or another except her."

"Yes," Radliegh said. "Amalie is not without her insights."

"I am not accusing your wife, in particular."

"Do you accuse my children? As you no doubt

have surmised, I am familiar with my children's passions, to whatever extent you are familiar with them."

"Doctor Radliegh, you have created a most unusual environment here at Vindemia."

"Unusual?" Through his horn-rimmed glasses, Radliegh blinked at the ceiling. "Isn't it the ideal environment, for my employees, friends, family that anyone would create if he could? Aren't you enjoying your stay at Vindemia, Mister Fletcher?"

"You've created a dictatorship."

"Weren't you taught in school that the best form of governance is a benign dictatorship?"

"I was taught dictatorships do not remain benign long."

"Mine has. I do not have to collect taxes. Quite the reverse. I do not have to conscript for wars."

"But you do make demands. You are shoving one son into politics, another into business administration, a daughter into movie stardom—"

"I have every right to make demands. Look at all I have provided them. Having received so much, they must give, not to me, but to the world. The formula is simple." Radliegh shook his left hand as if to get water off it. "I hate second generations which squander their resources."

"Do I have to recite to you the results of your forcing this 'formula,' as you call it—"

"I know, I know. My daughter, Alixis, forced herself into your son's bed last night."

"She did?"

"There must be something magnetic about your son."

"He plays the guitar."

"I've heard him. He plays well. I suppose a young man who concentrates on the use of his fingers has a certain superficial sexual appeal."

Fletch sighed. Having had only a sip of cognac, he was feeling uncommonly tired.

It had been a long day.

Too long to end it intellectually wrestling with a certified genius.

"And my football hero, Phi Beta Kappa son, Chet, is screwing the boy next door. Next door to your son, that is. And I've arranged rehabilitation for Duncan, which will begin Monday, in a cottage here at Vindemia."

"And your thrice married daughter is blackmailing you."

"It's the maturing process, Mister Fletcher. These days."

"Is that the way you see it?"

"Certainly. Childish rebellion. They do everything they know is abhorrent to me. Unfortunately, I gave them nothing to rebel against . . . except me. I am prayerfully waiting for them to grow up, mature, develop the appreciation, respect, and usefulness I expect from them."

"Will you live to see it?"

"They have the best chance of surviving here at Vindemia." The light on Radliegh's glasses prevented Fletch from seeing his eyes. "They shall grow up. They have to."

"Doctor Radliegh, someone murdered, by mistake, we think, Doctor Jim Wilson."

"I will not hear one word against my family, not my wife, my mother-in-law, my sons or daughters. What you and your son have learned here you are to carry away in silence, or I guarantee you . . ."

"What?"

"Or your son will go back to federal prison again for a crime he did not commit, only this time he will spend his life there. I can arrange it."

"I'm sure you can."

"Nevertheless, in the morning, we shall enjoy the Bierstadt together. I do appreciate your book. And your well-meant efforts on my behalf."

"Eric Beauville—"

Radliegh raised the palm of his right hand to the vertical. "Enough! I feel about my employees as I feel about my family."

"It's how they feel about you, idiot, that matters."

Radliegh laughed. "I've never been called an idiot before. How refreshing."

"Sorry. You are exasperating. You are not God, Doctor Radliegh."

"I've been told that before. I have never made such a claim. I do not think of myself as such. It's just that . . ."

"What?"

"If one has certain large capacities . . ."

"Why not use them to control people of lesser capacities? Is that it?"

"Why not use them to help others fulfill themselves? That's all I'm doing, Mister Fletcher. For example, you were about to mention Eric Beauville. No one else would have him as Chief Executive Officer. He's a second-rate brain with second-rate energies: a number two man. He thinks he'd be happier somewhere else. He wouldn't be."

"So you block his every effort to get away from you."

"For his own good, and the good of his family. He and they are much happier here than they would be anywhere else. And far more prosperous. And," Radliegh said with a smile, "keeping him here keeps him down to only two cigars a day."

Fletch shook his head. "Well, Jack asked me to talk with you. I've talked with you."

Radliegh nodded. "Thanks for coming."

Fletch put his brandy snifter on the desk. He hesitated. "Whoever killed Doctor Jim Wilson is going to be discovered. I guarantee you that."

"I have arranged for an investigation by the Georgia Bureau of Investigation. A Lieutenant Corso is due here tonight."

"You spent this much time picking a man you can control. Right?"

Radliegh said, "One way or another, Mister Fletcher, in this matter I shall see that justice is done. See you in the morning. At seven in the gymnasium?"

"Okay." Fletch headed toward the door.

"Mister Fletcher?"

Fletch turned.

Standing where he was when Fletch first entered the room, Radliegh said, "One moment please." He paused. "Mister Fletcher, I am about to have a massive coronary occlusion."

"What?"

Radliegh fell forward. His chest, head hit the edge of the side of the desk. He continued falling sideways. As he fell to the floor, the globe of the world fell over.

He lay on his back between the desk and the toppled globe.

Fletch said, "My God!"

He rushed forward.

Lifting the globe aside, he knelt on one knee beside Radliegh.

Radliegh's eyelids fluttered. Then were still.

Fletch felt for a pulse in Radliegh's neck, then his left wrist.

Aloud, Fletch said, "You were right again, Radliegh."

21

"Jack?"

Leaving the door open, Fletch had entered Jack's half of the cottage in the dark and turned on the bedside lamp.

Jack sat up straight on the bed and squinted at Fletch.

"What time is it?" he asked.

"Quarter to one."

Jack shook his head. "I was asleep."

Fletch said, "That's a good way to spend time in bed, too."

"What's the matter?" Jack asked. "You're still in black tie."

"Radliegh's dead."

"Doctor Chester Radliegh?"

"The one and only."

"Who killed him?"

"I did."

"What?"

Fletch said, "I killed Chester Radliegh."

"Tell me the one about why the turtle crossed the road."

"To get to the Shell station."

"You're kidding."

"Not kidding."

"You killed him with what? How?"

"Talk. You asked me to talk with him. I talked with him. I think you were right: no one has ever really talked with, at Chester Radliegh before. It was a stressful conversation. In retrospect, I realize I questioned his entire modus vivendi. I called him a dictator. I even called him an idiot."

"You called Doctor Chester Radliegh an idiot?"

"It just slipped out. An obdurate man, no matter how brilliant, is an idiot."

"Calling him an idiot killed him?"

"He had a massive coronary occlusion. He said no one had ever called him an idiot before."

"A heart attack."

"Yes."

"He was poisoned."

"No. I was alone in the room with him. We drank from the same bottle of cognac. He had a heart attack. Even he knew it was a heart attack. His own doctor was at the party. He has said Radliegh died of a heart attack."

"He died of a heart attack."

"You're getting it."

"You didn't kill him."

"I hate obduracy."

Jack said, "I hate French fries that look like pubic hair."

Fletch said, "That's real interesting. A detective named Corso has arrived from the Georgia Bureau of Investigation."

"Already?"

"He's not here to investigate Radliegh's death. I gather he was handpicked by Radliegh to investigate the murder of Doctor Jim Wilson."

"What good is it to handpick a detective?"

"Well, suppose the detective discovers the murderer is a member of the family, or whoever. Given enough power and influence, a deal can be made whereby that person is spirited away into a sanatorium, for example, and never brought to trial . . ."

"That's possible?"

"It's been known to happen."

"Why would Radliegh want to protect anyone who tried to kill him?"

"I've just conversed with the late Doctor Radliegh."

"I know. I've already sworn to myself to be less obdurate with you."

"That's good."

"I learn fast."

"He was highly protective of his family, no matter what they did. They could do no wrong, at least as far as the public was concerned. He insisted all their crimes and misdemeanors, including many alleged efforts to do him in, were just growing pains, signs of youthful rebelliousness."

"They weren't."

"He seemed to deny their true natures. Or believe they would overcome their true natures, given time."

"Didn't saints believe that?"

"His pride went so far as to believe they, no one, would succeed in hurting him. And his evidence, derived by what he called scientific method, was that none had succeeded, yet."

"He felt that because they hadn't succeeded in killing him they didn't really, deeply intend to kill him? All these attempts were just Freudian slips??"

"Something like that."

"And then you came along."

"To succeed where others fail...." Fletch cleared his throat. "At his last moment, if he was using anything like the scientific method I learned, he may have seen the light."

Jack said, "Pride cometh before a fall."

"Amen."

"He fell."

"Onto the globe of his world."

Through the soft lamplight surrounding the bed, Jack was squinting toward the open door of his quarters.

Barefoot, wearing only boxer shorts with horses' heads stamped on them in red, Peppy stood there. "What's happened?" he asked. "Who's this?"

Jack said, "My father."

Peppy looked at the older man in black tie and white summer formal jacket beside the bed and then at the naked young man in the bed. "Oh."

Baldly, Jack said, "Doctor Radliegh died of a heart attack."

"A heart attack?"

"Natural causes," Fletch said.

"Are you sure?" Peppy asked.

"I'm sure."

"Oh, shit," Peppy said. "Shit, shit, shit."

"Amen," Fletch said.

"Now the shit hits the fan," Peppy said.

"Who—?"

Lying in bed on his side in the pitch black room, Jack awoke startled. Fingers were laced behind his neck. In his sleep his right knee had moved forward and discovered a smooth thigh.

He worked his hips and legs backward in the bed. "Alixis?"

"Alixis?" Shana asked.

"Shana."

"Chester's dead."

"I know." The tips of his fingers touched her cheeks wet with tears. "I'm sorry."

"Just hold me, Jack. Okay?"

"Okay."

"Hold me tight."

"Okay."

• • •

"Hello?"

"Fletch?"

"Yes, Crystal."

"I'm sorry to call you at such an ungodly hour."

"I'm awake." Sitting on the edge of his bed, Fletch looked around at the walls of the bedroom of the Monkey Grass Suite on the third floor of the main house at Vindemia. The walls were papered with the ground cover.

"Jack all right?"

"He's fine. He'll call you in the morning."

"Fletch?"

"Yes, Crystal?"

"I think I'm hungry."

"Oh."

"I'm lying in the corner of this huge gym in the dark. For some reason, the reading lamp doesn't work. I think Mister Mortimer rigged it. Do you suppose he might have rigged it?"

"He's a mean man."

"I can't even read."

"So try sleeping, for once."

"All he left me to get through the night was a tall glass of skim milk."

"So take a sip and go to sleep."

"I drank it."

"All of it?"

"Hours ago."

"I see."

"Fletch, instead of sheep, I was counting plates of pasta. You know, tomato sauce. Tomato, meat sauce. Cheese. Garlic bread. When I began substituting broiled lobsters with drawn butter, I thought I had better call you."

"Right. They're more expensive."

"Baked lobsters stuffed with crab."

"Enough. You're making me hungry."

"Sorry. Misery proliferates."

"Believe it or not, you'll get through the night."

"Tell me again what I'm really feeling."

"It's not hunger."

"It feels like hunger."

"It's what you've always recognized as hunger, responded to as hunger."

"So what is it?"

"Digestive pangs."

"I'm feeling digestive pangs, not hunger pangs?"

"Believe it."

"Is it true?"

"How do I know? It's just an idea of mine. For now, I suspect you're better off believing it."

"Okay. I believe. Why are you awake so late?"

"Doctor Radliegh died after dinner."

"How? Did someone kill him?"

"Yeah. I did."

"How did you do that?"

"Just by talking to him."

"Mister Mortimer said no one should ever listen to you."

"He's right, I guess."

"Digestive pangs, not hunger pangs," she scoffed. "Who ever heard of such a thing? That's okay, Fletch. You can still talk to me."

Fletch couldn't help yawning. "Try to sleep, Crystal."

"Digestive pangs means I've eaten. That right?"

"That's right."

"Well," she sighed. "I guess I have. Good night, Fletch."

"Sleep tight. Don't let the lobsters bite."

"Thanks, Fletch."

Fletch yawned again. "Thanks died at Hialeah, or something."

"Jack?"

The full lengths of their bodies were on their sides facing each other tight together. He had held Shana through the night.

As still as something inanimate, she had wept silently.

At some point, not moving, Jack had fallen back asleep.

Now dawn light was in the windows.

"Jack? Make love to me gently? Softly? Slowly?"

"Are you sure you want me to?"

"Yes. Please."

It was full light when Jack was shaving in his little bathroom.

Shana's face appeared beside his left shoulder in the bathroom mirror.

Her eyes narrowed and turned hard.

She was looking at the scar on his back.

She said: "Alixis."

She disappeared from the mirror.

To his surprise, he heard his cottage door close before he had the soap off his face.

22

"This place will go to ruin in no time," Mrs. Houston said to Jack.

He could not disagree with her.

Vindemia was already ruined.

Confused, concerned, curious, Jack had bicycled around the estate after he had cooked and eaten a large breakfast alone in his cottage.

Although it was early Sunday morning there were cars coming and going on Vindemia's roads. And they were not maintaining the sedate speed limit. Nor were they all vehicles that belonged to the people who worked and lived on the estate. A few honked at him impatiently to get himself and his bike out of their way, off the road. An approaching car passing another sent him and his bike into a ditch.

The gates of Vindemia were open.

The guardhouse, which had stone walls a foot thick and sat in the middle of the double road, was empty. The telephone had been pulled from the wall and taken. When Jack had entered Vindemia he thought he had seen a small television in the guardhouse. There was none there now.

The gatehouse itself appeared empty. A first floor window had been smashed. Curtains flapped through an open second story window. The screen on the back door had been broken.

From there, Jack looked back at the main house, a mile away.

The ten huge blue and white flags were not waving from the roof of the house. No one had raised the flags, even to half mast.

Jack realized he had missed the sound of the flags snapping in the wind.

He rode to the village.

In the streets around the village cars were parked in front of nearly every house. A few cars were parked on the lawns immediately in front of houses. There were more children's toys scattered in the yards than there were children playing with them.

There were many cars and pickup trucks parked in front of the General Store. The woman who had been clerking the store stood on the porch in a housedress and slippers. She glanced at Jack when he pulled up on his bike. She had a coughing fit. Two men came out of the store carrying cases of groceries, passed her on the porch, went down the steps and packed the cases in the trunk of a small car.

On the sidewalk in front of the Recreation Center had been spray painted: GIMME SOME SUGAR, SANDY.

At the end of the street the digital clock in the tower whirred silently. The flag on the tower had not been raised.

Deducing easily, Jack rode to the vehicle compound.

The chain locking the gate had been cut through. The chain-link gate was open. The door to the shed had been kicked in.

Almost all the cars, except Jack's, were gone.

In the shed Jack found his own car keys hanging on a peg and pocketed them.

Only a few airplanes, the two small jets marked RADLIEGH MIRROR, the ancient two-seater, and another small corporate jet were still there. Jack had been hearing the planes of party guests taking off much of the morning, even before dawn.

There were no cars in the parking lot of the office building.

He rode around the country club. There were many cars parked there. Sunday midmorning it sounded as if a party were raging. Jack smelled pork barbecue smoking. Golf carts were lined up at the first tee like toll booth traffic. There were more brightly clad people stirring around the country club than Jack knew were on Vindemia.

He watched teen-agers racing golf carts. The youngsters were trying to brake and spin the golf carts simultaneously to cut up the lawn. One racing golf cart nearly tipped over on the slope surrounding the swimming pool. That caused a laugh.

Biking back toward the main house, Jack found Mrs. Houston walking on the green verge along the side of the road. She carried a thick brown walking stick. She was not using it to walk.

Jack stopped his bike to talk with her. They were in the shade of the deciduous trees spaced along the sides of the road.

"You know," she said, "when we first came here, when Chester was first beginning to build Vindemia, he tried to run a garden of his own. I guess I talked him into it.

"He couldn't do it.

"He built a tight fence around it that went down three feet into the ground and six feet into the air, put a gate on it, and locked it. I asked him if he thought rabbits and deer and groundhogs have degrees in engineering.

"He watered it twice a day. Every day he gave it fertilizer. There was no such thing as a weed in that garden. As soon as I knew what he was doing, I told him to stop, leave it alone. Every time a plant looked peakish, he replaced it.

"He spoiled it. He killed it with care."

While they talked, a pickup truck came along the road. Two men rode in front. A third stood in back.

There were two rifles in a rack in the truck's rear window.

The truck was going slowly.

The two men in front waved at them.

As the truck passed, the man standing in back

smiled down at them. He said to them, "Sure is a pretty place you have here."

Neither Mrs. Houston nor Jack waved, smiled, or answered.

As the truck went around the curve an empty beer can thrown from it hit the pavement and rattled until it ran out of momentum.

Glancing at Mrs. Houston, Jack saw her cheeks wet with tears.

"Chester was that way," Mrs. Houston said. "He thought about what people wanted, to be happy and healthy, needed, to fulfill themselves and be useful, and he provided it with an open hand. He protected them, even from themselves, if you know what I mean. And instead of getting back pleasure in their strength, happiness, accomplishments, some respect, appreciation, all he got back was envy, resentment, anger, hatred, everybody's desire to destroy him or see him destroyed.

"He had to give up on his flower garden.

"Why didn't he learn from it?"

23

"**H**ere he is now," Fletch said.

As Jack rode his bike under the oriole of Vindemia's main house, he found Fletch and another man strolling the driveway from the other direction. Jack did not recognize the other man.

"Jack," Fletch said, "this is Lieutenant Corso of the Georgia Bureau of Investigation."

Straddling his bike in the shade of the oriole, Jack shook hands with the man.

"I've been telling the Lieutenant everything I know about what's been going on here." Fletch looked up from lowered eyebrows at Jack. "I told him you would do the same."

Corso studied Jack's shorts. "You work here?"

"Yes, sir."

"Blue and white, blue and white: everything around here is blue and white." He looked down at his trousers. "I'm glad I wore my green suit."

Jack said, "The flags aren't up."

"I've never seen such a place as this. Didn't know such a place existed."

"I have," Fletch said. "Several. The man who builds such a place thinks he's building it for his family to enjoy forever."

"The gates are open," Jack said.

Vehicles were passing the house slowly.

"I've been telling the Lieutenant about the lethal gas," Fletch said. "That there wasn't supposed to be any such thing in the laboratory. It must have come from somewhere, put there by someone. We've just come back from the lab."

"Who knows?" Corso squinted. "Big lab like that. I don't recognize anything that's in it. All this paraphernalia. Who knows what's supposed to be there? It's all just junk to me. Anybody could have put anything in there at any time. The guy himself—what's his name, Wilson?—could have drug it in himself. I used to have a chem teacher in high school, he'd take a few whiffs of something during the lunch hour. I saw him do it."

Fletch glanced at Jack from an even more low-ered face. He sighed.

"Well, I guess I should go question people," Corso said. "About all these alleged accidents, horses falling over, frayed coffeepot wires, you say have been happening around here. You guys want to come with me? I mean, you guys can pick it up if someone says somethin' you know not to be true from somethin' you saw or heard, or somethin'. You know what I mean?"

"Sure," Fletch said.

"I asked for people to be in the living room." Corso opened the enormous brass-studded front door to the house.

Jack leaned his bike against a column.

He asked his father, "This guy any good?"

Fletch said, "If he were any stupider he'd need a bar code."

They followed Corso into the house.

"Freedom is the opportunity for self-discipline," Fletch said. "Let's see if anyone around here is an opportunist."

"Who said that?" Jack asked.

"Fellow named General Eisenhower. Maybe he said, 'Democracy is the opportunity for self-discipline.' "

"You mean President Eisenhower?"

"You know this lawyer, Nicolson?" Fletch asked.

"No," Jack said.

"Apparently Radliegh's personal lawyer. He got called in yesterday from Atlanta. It seems yesterday morning Radliegh suddenly wanted to review his Last Will and Testament."

"I know that to be true," Jack said. "I heard Beauville and Radliegh's secretary talking about it."

The living room actually was several living rooms, or large sitting areas, each large enough to seat twenty or more people comfortably, in one huge room.

"Homey," Fletch commented. "Makes me want to ask when my flight to Tulsa leaves."

"Do airlines still give out that kind of information?" Jack asked.

"Not voluntarily," Fletch answered. "Or reliably."

In one living area Beauville, Downes, and a third man Jack assumed was Nicolson stood in a group near the fireplace, the center of attention. On Sunday morning each wore a proper gray suit and tie.

Mrs. Amalie Radliegh, in black dress, hat and gloves, sat in a wing-back chair. A black veil covered her face.

The Radliegh children sat as separated from each other as they could be in that space.

Daughter Amy MacDowell sat in another wing-back chair, suckling an infant.

In black shorts, Alixis sprawled on one divan; in khaki slacks and blue button-down shirt, Chet sat a little straighter in another.

Duncan, not shaven, hair uncombed, sat on the carpet in greasy overalls and t-shirt.

Nancy Dunbar sat on the divan with Chet.

Mrs. Houston was not there. Jack had just seen her on the road.

Nor was Shana Staufel there. Jack had heard her leave his cottage shortly after dawn.

"Oh, Jack . . ." Alixis looked up at him through tear sodden eyes. "I lost my daddy."

Jack said, "I never heard such crap."

Nicolson was talking to them all. "All I am saying is that there is plenty of money, of course. The estate will be settled. Each of you will be very well off. But . . ."

"But what?" Chet asked.

"But this is a surprise to us all. A terrible surprise."

Duncan scoffed.

Downes said, "It's a huge estate."

"With huge problems," Beauville said.

"No," Nicolson countered. "There shouldn't be any real problems."

"Of course there are," Beauville said. "There always are."

"As you know," Nicolson said, "your dad was a very well organized man."

Jack saw Fletch watching Corso. The Lieutenant evinced no intention of breaking in, taking control of this discussion, beginning his questioning. He seemed to have settled in his brown shoes and green trousers like a cop on a corner content to watch the human comedy.

Alixis sniffed loudly.

"But he was reasonably young and very healthy and did not know he was going to die last night," Nicolson said.

"What is your point?" Chet asked.

The baby at Amy's breast slurped.

"Settling this estate is going to take a lot of time," Nicolson said. "Two, three years, at least."

"While you lawyers dine out on it," Alixis said.

"Right," Chet said. "While you each make your life's fortune off it. You'll take the rest of our lives to settle the estate. Build your hours. Generate paperwork. Misfile papers. Make wrong motions. You won't get away with it. I won't let you."

Duncan said, "How much do I get? When do I get it? I've got things to do."

Alixis said, "Duncan, we all want to get away from here."

From behind her veil, Mrs. Radliegh inquired, "Do any of you intend to stay for the funeral?"

Jack heard a noise behind him and turned around.

Shana stood there.

Her face looked like that of an eagle. Her eyes seemed entirely protruding pupils. Her jaw was set to hold a beak.

Standing behind Fletch, Corso and Jack, she was looking around them, watching the people in the living area, listening to them.

She did not glance at Jack's face.

Amalie Radliegh said, "I think we should bury him out by the laundry yard. You know, where the maids air out the sheets?"

"The point is," Nicolson said, "there is only one hundred thousand dollars in available cash."

Alixis gasped. "A hundred thousand dollars?"

"It's mine," Duncan said loudly. "I have to have it for my new racing car!"

"Like hell, Duncan," Amy said. "My children come first!"

"I already owe eighty five thousand dollars!" Duncan said.

Amy resettled the baby at her breast. "My children are the only grandchildren of Chester Radliegh. They come first. And they always will."

Amalie Radliegh said, "You know how Chester always liked his sheets aired out."

Alixis said, "To hell with you both. I need to set up a place in California."

Duncan said, "I don't care what any of you say. I need to pay this bill, or the car won't get finished in time to race."

"Now you'll all get allowances from the estate," Nicolson said. "Adequate allowances. It will take a little while to set them up."

"Allowance," Chet said. "Lot of good that will do. You mean us all to stay here?"

"Why not?" Downes asked. "Until things get set up."

"Well, I claim the apartment in New York," Chet said. "And the rest of you can stay out."

"No one wants to live with you, Chet baby," Alixis said. "But I do need to buy a place in Malibu. I've been promising it to myself."

Red-faced, Beauville seemed to be talking to the floor. "Well, I'm fed up for sure. Don't look to me to run the company. I'm gone as soon as I get a decent offer."

A telephone rang. Nancy Dunbar reached from the divan and answered it. "Hello?"

"We've all suffered enough, this place. Everybody spying," Alixis said.

"I see." Nancy Dunbar hung up. She had not said, "I'll take care of it."

Nancy said, "A child was just run over outside the General Store. Hit by a car. A six-year-old boy. He was killed."

"To hell with your brats!" Duncan exploded at Amy. "And you!" he said to Alixis. "It would be good to be rid of you. Talk about spyin'! But you're not taking my money just to build yourself a human stud farm in Malibu!"

Alixis snickered. "Oouh. How'd you guess?"

"Damned nympho," Duncan said.

"Druggy," Alixis said.

"Where is Chester now?" Amalie Radliegh asked. "Where did they put him?"

"I don't know what to say to you all," Nicolson said.

"You've said it all." Chet stood up. "I'm going. I'll leave the jet at the Atlanta airport, if anybody cares."

"We need some cooperation here, a little under-standing." Nicolson was pleading. "We've got to find a way of being fair!"

Then Shana stepped around Fletch, Corso, and Jack. She moved toward the center of the living area.

Her face was as red as the setting sun.

"You murderers!" she screamed. Her right fist was up. "You're all murderers! Every one of you! Each one of you murdered Chester as surely as if you had driven a knife through his heart!"

Chet looked at her curiously.

"Ah, shut up," Duncan said.

"Why is she yelling?" Amalie Radliegh said. "She'll wake the dead."

To Amalie Radliegh, Shana said, "You did everything you could to make him miserable, every minute. You never tried to understand him! You just stayed in your room, taking pills, drinking by yourself, weeping, telling everybody how miserable you are! Love? Hell! You never even took responsibility. Did you ever try to teach your children to respect their father? To understand him?"

"I never understood him myself," Amalie said. "It was too much work. Well, it was impossible. The man would talk about anything from ants to spaceships."

"Did you ever listen to him?"

"I did. At first. It wore me out. Are there ants in space, do you suppose? They're everywhere else."

In a lower voice, hands on hips, Shana said, "You've all been trying to kill Chester. Each and every damned one of you."

"I haven't," Amy said. "I've made my life." To Nicolson she asked, "There's no way Vindemia is to be sold, is there?"

"Who'd buy it?" Duncan asked. "Who'd want it?"

Beauville answered, "I expect new corporate officers will want to move headquarters out of here. Who wants to live in this hellhole?"

"I do," Amy said. "My children do. I expect this place to continue."

"You'll be mighty lonely here," Chet said.

"There's Mother," Amy said. "She'll stay. Where could she go?"

"That's what I mean," Chet said. "You'll be mighty lonely."

"Paying the servants comes first," Nicolson said.

"Three have already resigned," Nancy Dunbar said.

"They have?" Downes asked.

"They're waiting for their checks in the kitchen," she said. "I forgot to tell you."

"Nobody's writing any checks on that money!" Duncan said. "I have an emergency. I wrote Dad a memo."

"I saw it," said Downes. "For a college graduate you don't spell worth shit."

"You have nothing to say about it, Downes!"

"Sloppiest thing I ever saw. I can't believe Vanderbilt sells degrees. How did you get a college degree, Duncan?"

Chet said, "I'm gone."

"You are the most horrible people!" Shana's eyes were closed. "None of you deserves anything! You never gave Chester a moment of peace! You never appreciated him as much as did his dog!"

"I appreciate him now," Amy said. "He's dead."

"Freedom with moola." Alixis stretched. "No one to tell me what to do."

"He always made me feel like shit," Duncan said.

"No one could be as good as he was."

"You made yourself feel like shit!" Shana said. "You are shit! Worthless shit! None of you is worth one hair of Chester's head."

"Where is Arky?" Amalie asked. "I haven't seen him around all morning."

"I shot him," Duncan said. "I've been looking forward to doing that."

"You have no idea," Shana continued as if talking to herself, "how hard he worked, how much he did for you, tried to do for you, how much he wanted for you, how much he loved you."

"Sure, sure," Alixis said, "as long as we met all his demands."

"If there were justice . . ." Eyes still closed, Shana rocked a little on her feet. "There'd be a bus outside the front door to cart you all off to prison. You're all murderers, as sure as God made little green apples."

Fists tight at her side, head down, Shana turned to leave the room into the foyer.

"You're the one that's leaving, Shana old girl. Don't hesitate." Clumsily, Duncan lifted himself off the floor into a standing position. "Chet seems to be leaving without you. Did you notice?"

"Justice . . ." Shana said.

Amalie said, "We haven't decided yet where to plant Chester. Who votes for near the laundry yard? I hate gravestones where you can't help seeing them."

Getting up, Alixis said, "I'm packin' my bikinis.

Down payment on a Malibu house will take more than a hundred grand."

His finger in her face, Duncan shouted at her, "I told you that's my money!"

"Oh, stick it up your nose, Duncan."

"He would." Rearranging her brassiere, Amy said, "That money goes to paying the servants and keeping this place running. There's Grandmother to think of."

"Sure," Duncan said. "You're thinking of senile old Grandmother. It would be a little cheaper to put her in a nursery, don't you think, cow? You we can put in the dairy." To Nicolson, Duncan said, "My father planned for me to run this show. I'm taking that money."

"As a matter of fact," Beauville said, "your father planned for you to start rehab tomorrow."

Duncan's face drained of the little pallor it had. "Like hell."

"Sure," Alixis said. "I'm sure he had plans for all of us. Plans and plans and plans." Leaving the room, she said, "Well, he's dead. So are his plans. Thank God."

Angrily, Duncan grabbed an end table and tossed it on its side. The lamp on it smashed. "Get me out of here!" Leaving, he stumbled over the table's legs.

Saying nothing, Amy carried her baby out of the room.

Ashen, Nicolson and Downes remained standing as they were. Beauville was florid.

"Has anything been decided?" Amalie asked from behind her veil.

"Not a damned thing," Nicolson said. "Except that you sure have four disrespectful, self-centered brats."

"That's good," Amalie said. "I'm feeling tired now." Uncertainly, she stood up and headed out of the room. "I'm doing well not to weep."

Downes asked Dunbar, "What kid got run over?"

"You see," Beauville said to Nicolson, "the children here aren't used to there being cars on the roads. Shows you how stupid this place is."

Still sitting on the couch, Nancy Dunbar spoke to Beauville. "I guess I've had it with this place, myself. I wasn't sure until I just heard these people. I can't stand it anymore. I guess I'll leave today, too."

"Oh, that's great!" Beauville said angrily. "Leave me completely in the lurch!"

"I don't think I care." On high heels, Nancy Dunbar began leaving the room. "Unlike everyone else around here, I guess I've got what I want."

Corso said to Fletch, "I guess this wasn't a good time to question these folks."

"You'll never get them together again. Never."

"I don't know what they had to say, anyway."

"Seems to me we heard quite a lot," Jack said.

"Laboratory accident," Corso said. "That gas could have been there for years. That's the easiest answer."

"Are you looking for the easiest answer?" Fletch asked.

"Somebody had to arrange to release the gas," Jack said.

"Yeah, well. Maybe."

"Coming for lunch?" Jack asked Fletch.

"Lunch. Can you do lunch?"

"Sandwiches," Jack said. "Cheese."

"I'll be at your place in a few minutes. I think I saw a date on the label of that gas canister. I'll just go back to the lab and check it."

"Yeah," Corso said. "You do that. Let me know."

24

As Fletch walked back from the laboratory passing the main house, his pocket phone buzzed.

"Hello?" On the driveway in front of the house he stopped to listen.

"Fletch . . ."

"Hi, Crystal. How are you doing this morning? Did you survive the night?"

"I slept."

"That's good."

"There must have been something in the milk."

"That was the milk. By itself. It's the best sedative."

"I've had a breakfast of only grapefruit juice with protein powder in it, one coffee, vitamins and an amino acid tablet called L-Carnitine. Well, I had the tablet before breakfast."

"That's nice."

"I feel very energetic. I've done a total of five sit-ups already this morning, and used the ankle and wrist weights a total of twenty minutes."

"You'll sleep tonight."

A small jet airplane taking off from Vindemia's airstrip roared over Fletch's head.

Fletch looked up at it.

The plane was marked RADLIEGH MIRROR.

He assumed it was Chet Radliegh leaving Vindemia, his family, his fiancée, leaving well before the funeral of his father.

"How did you get workmen to come to this Godforsaken place on a Sunday morning?" Crystal asked.

"I didn't. What workmen?"

"They're replacing the mirrors here in the gym with perfect mirrors. They said the order came from I. M. Fletcher. I do believe you are I.M.?"

"I am," Fletch said. "It did. But I didn't ask that the mirrors be delivered Sunday morning."

"Well, they're here. The workmen showed up about eight o'clock. They've been working all morning."

"That's nice," Fletch said. "Guess I'll be paying time-and-a-half or double-time, or something."

"Maybe not," Crystal said. "Maybe they know about you. Maybe they heard about what you did to that terrible place, Blythe Spirit."

"Beg pardon?"

Under the sound of the jet engine, Fletch had to strain to hear Crystal.

"Blythe Spirit was a terrible place, Fletch." Crystal's voice was low. "I'm glad you got me out of there. All their expensive, expert help had succeeded only in making me hopeless. I'm glad you nailed those bastards."

"Is Mister Mortimer pleased?" Fletch asked. "I mean, with the new mirrors?"

"He'll never tell you. No, in fact he's been expostulating all morning. First, at the boys' training schedule being interrupted. The next explosion from his mouth was, 'Why doesn't that Fletcher mind his own damned business?' Then, when he watched Ricky seeing himself for the first time in the floor-to-ceiling, wall-to-wall perfect mirrors, he fumed. 'Now that damned boy won't want to fight anybody but himself, ever! For a boy fightin' himself in a mirror I couldn't sell a ticket to a nun,' was what he said. I noticed he didn't send the mirrors back, though."

"I can always tell when he's pleased."

"Ricky is why I'm calling."

"Ricky? The younger boy? Why would you be calling me about him?"

"I've discovered him."

"Was he under a rock?"

"You know *Leaves of Grass?*"

"Whitman. Of course."

"No, 'Leaves of grass, grains of sand/ Seasoned, soldier, hardened man/ Is what I'm told I am . . . '?"

"Guess I missed that one."

"I found it in an anthology here. I just read it to him. To Ricky. Because they couldn't work out in the gym this morning, with your workmen here.

Listen to this. I'm putting him on."

"Crystal—" At that moment, Fletch did not expect to be listening to a sixteen-year-old boxer in Montana recite poetry to him by long-distance telephone.

Then Fletch heard Ricky speaking. To him. To his core.

" 'Leaves of grass, grains of sand//Seasoned soldier, hardened man / Is what I'm told I am.' "

Through Fletch's little telephone came Ricky's magnificently timbred, modulated voice enhanced by his distinct diction, thrilling cadence: " 'Drinking mud, eating grass: / Think of me as Saddam's ass. // We're of different centuries / You and I. / I'm taught to think of lips for lips, / Eye for eye, / While you, my conqueror, are trained / To think of blips; / Coordinate hand, eye and brain . . .' "

Fletch stuck his index finger in his opposite ear and hunched over a little to hear better.

The voice was compelling. " 'Moslem, Christian and Jew / You do not know me as a man, / A true believer in Saddam, / See my bravery, see me bleed. / Even my final, dying scream: / Silent on your computer screen . . .' " In the voice of this sixteen-year-old boxer in Montana was a touch of the best, some of the surety, authority, timbre, rhythmic sense of Olivier, Burton . . .

To himself, Fletch mouthed: "Wow!"

Hunched over, finger in his ear, listening to Ricky over a cheap telephone speaking more than a thousand miles away, Fletch felt something electrical go up his spine and burst in the back of his head between his ears.

" 'The bazaar battled the arcade, / And, naturally, the arcade won. / You've had the benefits of our oil, / While my mother and I have had none. // The problem is, and think of this, / It is your every wish / To drag me into a new time, / The century of bliss. / While the world economy thins / Resources shall be averaged. / It matters not who wins. // Seasoned soldier, hardened man / Is what I'm told I am. / You, the pinball wizard mind, / The tommy deaf, dumb, and blind.' "

There was a pause. Then the boy's voice, not speaking into the telephone, asked, "All right, Mrs. Faoni?"

Crystal took the phone. "Fletch? Did you hear?"

"Yes."

"Are you hearing what I'm hearing?"

"That's some fine instrument that boy has."

"Fletch, Ricky isn't a boxer. He's an actor."

"Oh, Crystal! Mister Mortimer will kill you for sure."

Looking up at the house, Fletch wasn't sure what he was seeing.

"I read this poem to Ricky once, just once, this morning, and after a moment he began reciting it back to me, the whole thing, sounding as you just heard. Consider not only his sound. He'd memorized the whole thing only hearing it once! He still hasn't read it! Isn't he marvelous?"

"Outstanding."

Someone was tying a sheet, a white bedsheet, to a railing of one of the upper balconies.

He could not see who that someone was.

Sheets. Something about sheets.

Bedsheets wouldn't be aired from a balcony of the main house.

There was a laundry yard somewhere for that.

"Crystal, you can't take one of Mister Mortimer's two remaining boxers."

"Such talent can't be ignored. This boy should have his head beat in? No way! I won't have it. I think it's a very good thing you brought me here, Fletch. Who'd think of discovering a talented actor in boxing gloves and britches in Where-the-hell-am-I, Wyoming?"

"Why does that surprise you?" For a moment, nothing was happening on the balcony. The rest of the sheet did not appear. "What are you going to do about it, anyway, Crystal? I mean, do about him?"

"Work with him a little myself. I don't know much, but I know more about this than Mister Mortimer does. I'll read to him, make him read the texts, ask him what things mean, how he interprets them. I'll get some tapes, play them for him. This boy has never seen or heard anything other than Terminator movies. I'll get in touch with some people I know in regional theater—"

A black bulk appeared laid out along the top of the balcony railing. The bulk was as long as a person.

The black bulk rolled, was rolled off the railing.

As it fell, as the sheet unfurled, the body's arms extended above its head.

The lower end of the sheet was knotted around the neck of the bulk, of the body, of the person.

Fletch yelled: "Crystal! I'm seeing someone being hung!"

"What?"

Hanging from the balcony railing by a bedsheet tied around her neck, the body was swinging. The legs and arms struggled, but not much.

The black hat fell off the head and floated to the ground.

No head appeared over the railing.

"Mrs. Radliegh!" Fletch yelled into the phone. "Amalie! She's being hung! Good bye!"

Fletch was already running toward the house. As he ran, he folded his phone and tried without success to jam it into his pocket.

He jumped up steps and across a terrace into an enormous sunroom.

"I've been stabbed!"

Wearing only the bottom of a bikini, Alixis stood with Amy in the sunroom.

Alixis kept whirring around in a small circle, first this way, then that, whimpering, like a puppy chasing its tail. As she twisted, first she would reach her back with the fingers of one hand, then the other.

Each time she took her hand from her back she stared incredulously at the blood on her fingers.

There was blood on the floor where she was rotating on bare feet.

Amy was pacing around her sister, trying to examine her back. "Stay still! You haven't been stabbed! You've been cut by a barbecue fork!"

There were two wobbling parallel lines across Alixis' back dripping blood.

"Who did this to you?"

Amy said to Fletch, "I was asleep by the pool. Someone whacked me on the head——"

Fletch was dashing through the room. "Someone's hanging from a balcony."

"What?" Amy started to follow Fletch.

Alixis shrieked after them: "I'm bleeding!"

"Oh, shut up!" Amy yelled. "It's time somebody barbecued you, you fuckin' worthless piece of meat!"

Followed by Amy, Fletch ran up two wide staircases.

On the third floor, he opened the door of a room and looked through it. There was no bedsheet tied to the railing.

"Are you crazy?" Amy asked.

Pushing by her in the doorway, Fletch said, "I think it's your mother."

Amy followed him down the corridor. "I know she's crazy."

The next door to the left was open.

Fletch sprinted through the room onto the balcony.

A bedsheet was tied to the railing.

He looked over the balcony.

Less than four feet below the railing hung Amalie Radliegh. Her black hat and veil were on the ground way below her, but she still wore her long black dress and gloves.

Her face was purple.

Fletch supposed her neck was broken.

Her body hung limp.

Amy peered over the high railing like a child looking off a bridge. "Mother . . . ?"

"Sorry." Fletch turned Amy away from the sight.

There was the sound of a loud engine roaring somewhere on the estate.

At first Fletch thought it was the sound of another airplane lifting off.

"Is she dead?" An old woman came onto the balcony from the bedroom.

"Oh, Gran." Amy tried to put her arms around the old woman but was shrugged off.

"Are you Mrs. Houston?" Fletch asked. "Her mother?"

"Yes. Is she dead?"

"Yes."

Mrs. Houston did not look over the railing. "Once death starts happening, you see. . . . She did not hang herself."

"No," Fletch answered. "I don't think so."

"Oh, I know so. Amalie was miserable because she did not love and did not hate and did not hope and did not despair. She was murdered. Are you going to haul her up?"

The engine noise seemed at a distance but was still deafening.

Looking out over the estate, Amy said, "Duncan . . ."

"Yes," Mrs. Houston said. "Duncan is using his racing car to chase the locals off Vindemia. At least, that's what he thinks he's doing. His eyes are glazed with some fantasy. The local boys seem to be making sport of him. Which is why I came in."

Fletch asked, "Did you see your daughter hanging?"

Mrs. Houston began to choke, but stopped. "Yes. She was thrown off the railing, wasn't she?" The little woman made a pushing gesture with her hands. "Rolled off."

"I believe so."

"Amalie never had much fight in her. She never fought for anything she had, or was given her, to keep it, treasure it; not even her life."

"She'd probably taken some pills," Amy said. "Sedatives."

"I'm sure," Mrs. Houston said, "you are right."

"I'd better get Lieutenant Corso." Fletch started for the door to the bedroom.

For the first time he noticed the barbecue fork on the floor of the balcony. There was blood on the tips of the tines.

"No." Fletch stopped. He stared at the barbecue fork. "Amy, I think we had better go find your children. You both should come with me."

Then came the great explosion.

The sound of the roaring engine stopped instantly.

Fletch whipped around.

Even in the brilliant midday sunlight the white flames rising from the exploded racing car were visible a mile away.

The accident was in the middle of the road near the gatehouse.

The racing car had smashed into the guardhouse.

Below the flames Fletch saw what looked like pieces of a smashed mirror piled up against the stone wall.

Then great black smoke rose from the mirror fragments, and began to settle over the mess.

Amy said, "Oh, Duncan . . ."

Mrs. Houston sighed. She said, "And things could have been so nice, for everybody."

25

"**W**hat's that noise?" Peppy asked.

"Duncan," Jack answered.

When Jack had returned to his half of the cottage he found his door open.

Peppy was sitting on the sofa bed with a beer can in hand and four empties on the floor.

"I never heard that car make so much noise before, except on the track," Peppy said. Duncan's racing track was far from Vindemia's main buildings. "He's ridin' it around the estate roads at full throttle?"

"He's chasing people in pickup trucks."

"Chasing them!" Peppy's expression was wry. "What's he gonna do if he catches anybody? Cry in his face?"

"I'm making sandwiches for my father and me. How many do you want?"

"He'll whine at them. Complain about how life isn't fair. It's all his father's fault."

"How many sandwiches do you want?" Jack repeated. "Seeing you've made yourself at home, anyway."

"What kind of sandwiches?"

"Cheese. It's all I've got. How many?"

"Several."

"Running out of bread," Jack said. "This healthy bread comes in small packages."

"Jack, is your dad anything?"

"Anything like what?"

"Anything important. I mean, he was at that party last night."

"Journalist," Jack said.

"You mean, he's on television?"

"No," Jack said. "He's never been on television."

"Newspaper writer."

"Something like that."

" 'Cause I need help."

"You know Chet has left Vindemia?"

"Yes." Peppy shifted his booted feet on the floor. "And I'm not goin' to prison for that son of a bitch."

Jack was dealing sliced cheese on pieces of bread on the kitchenette counter. "What do you mean?"

"Will your dad be able to help me?"

"He may be able to."

"Chet got me to do somethin' I didn't want to do," Peppy said. "Somethin' I didn't know I was doin'."

"Sure," Jack said.

Peppy shrugged. "You don't know what I'm talkin' about."

"No," Jack said. "I don't."

"You find yourself doin' some ridiculous things around here."

"You've said that before."

"Have you found I tell you no lie?"

"I guess."

Peppy leaned forward. Elbows on his knees, he rubbed his eyes with the balls of his hands. "Chet told me he'd get up and go riding with his father on this particular morning. He'd be at the stables before dawn, have the horses saddled, surprise his old man, you know?"

"Yeah . . ." Doctor Radliegh sitting cross-legged in the woods, Arky the boxer dog in his lap, talking to Jack, saying he was "surprised" his children never went riding with him; he was "surprised" one morning Chet did go riding with him. . . .

"Want a beer?" Peppy asked.

Then there was the explosion.

"Jeez!" Jack jumped back from the counter. "What's that?"

Instantly the roaring sound of the engine stopped.

"Haw!" Peppy stood up. "Ol' Duncan just bought it." He hitched up his jeans. "Yes, sir. I do believe ol' Duncan just blew himself to hell and beyond." He smiled at Jack. "Probably blinded himself in that mirror car, again, wouldn't you guess?"

26

"**U**ndisciplined people are running amok," Jack said to Fletch.

"Or a disciplined person is running amok," Fletch said to Jack.

"Are we both right?" Jack asked.

Fletch said, "Empires crumble; then people, of all sorts, run amok."

A servant had told Jack and Peppy when they entered the main house that she had seen Mister Fletcher in the nursery when she happened to pass the open door. She gave them directions to the third floor, back of the building.

In the nursery's anteroom, Fletch sat in an easy chair.

The chair looked as if nurses and nannies, infants and small children, had lived in it: eaten in it, cuddled in it, played in it, slept in it.

Fletch looked unusually comfortable in the chair.

Through double doors a uniformed nanny and

Amy MacDowell were tending to the children.

Mrs. Houston sat in a rocking chair. Her hands were folded in her lap. Her face was turned toward the light from the windows.

"Jack," Fletch asked in a low, slow voice. "Can you tell me why someone would put two large cuts crosswise on Alixis Radliegh's back?"

"Did someone do that?" Jack asked.

"Yes. With a barbecue fork."

"Alixis doesn't know who?"

"She was on her stomach sunning on a pool lounge. She may have been asleep. She says someone hit her on the side of her head. When she became sensible, she found her back stinging and bleeding. At that point, she was alone in the pool area."

"You're asking me who would do that to Alixis?" Jack glanced at Peppy, who stood with half lidded eyes beside him. He looked like a horse going to sleep on his feet.

"And why."

Jack turned his back to his father. He pulled up his t-shirt.

"I see. Alixis did that to you?"

Turning around again, Jack said, "It isn't that important to me. It's just a cut."

"Did you see Duncan's accident?"

"Heard it," Jack said. "I don't need to see accidents."

Jack had the impression Fletch was still looking behind Jack.

And Fletch's voice continued low and slow.

"And I expect you saw Mrs. Radliegh hanging from the balcony."

"Yes." When Peppy saw the dangling corpse he puked into the driveway's gutter. "Why hasn't someone taken her down?"

"Lieutenant Corso is awaiting police reinforcements."

"Where is Lieutenant Corso now?"

"Went down to supervise the accident, I guess. Await reinforcements at the main gate."

"Do these events have anything to do with each other?"

"The barbecue fork was on the floor of the balcony from which Mrs. Radliegh was hung."

"Oh, no."

"Oh, yes."

"And you're sitting here alone in the nursery . . ."

"To protect Mrs. Houston, Amy Radliegh Mac-Dowell, and seven little Radliegh heirs."

"From." Jack said the word as if, by itself, it made a statement. He sucked in a big breath and let it go. Doing so did not cool his face. Fletch waited. Jack said, "Shana Staufel."

"I thought you'd think so, too." Fletch smiled. "I noticed the blood on your sheets. Chester Radliegh mentioned to me Alixis had shared your bed the night before. One of you had bled. I was willing to believe Alixis not a virgin. And, somehow, because a girl scratched your back in lovemaking, I couldn't see you attacking her with a barbecue fork; such smacks more of frustration, jealousy, than revenge." Very softly, slowly, Fletch said, "One might even speculate insanity. Nor could I see you threatening a drugged older woman with a barbecue fork, for any reason. Of course . . ." Fletch smiled again. He was giving his son time to think. "One can never be sure. Waiting for lab reports confirming Alixis' blood and Shana's fingerprints on the barbecue fork necessarily would have made me just a tad nervous. So I thought I'd ask."

Having thought, Jack said, "Shana's gone crazy."

Fletch shrugged. "Shana loved. She was so convinced people here were trying to kill the man she loved, she asked you to insinuate yourself into this household, and investigate. She convinced you that people here were trying to kill Chester Radliegh. You asked me to come here."

"They *were* trying to kill him."

"Be that as it may, they didn't. At least they didn't succeed. They may have driven him to his death, contributed to it. Shana may have been literally correct. Driving him to his death, his self-destruction, somehow, may have been their true intention."

Jack's eyes were big. "Shana killed Mrs. Radliegh."

"Mrs. Radliegh's suggestion of burying her accomplished husband in the laundry yard—such an expression of ignorance of and contempt for the man Shana loved deeply and passionately—rather tipped Shana over the edge, wouldn't you say?"

"So she hung Mrs. Radliegh with a bedsheet."

"After inscribing Alixis' back with a barbecue fork. She may have meant to do more harm to Alixis. Shana hit Alixis on the head hard enough to knock her momentarily senseless. Being inexpert in such matters, she may have thought she had killed Alixis."

"And you think Shana means harm to Amy?"

"Who knows what charges, real or imagined, Shana has against Amy, Mrs. Houston? Perhaps her mental state is such that she intends to deprive all natural heirs of Chester Radliegh from benefiting from his life, his work, his death. I decided I'd rather sit here than be sorry."

"She had nothing to do with Duncan's death, did she?"

"I think it will be found Duncan self-destructed. You see," Fletch said, "where Shana is wrong is in failing to understand the usual self-destructive nature of those eager to destroy others."

Again, Jack got the impression Fletch was talking to the side of his head, to the ceiling, walls behind him.

Jack's own eyes were attracted by the light in the nursery; his attention distracted by the noises and movements of the children.

"So," Fletch said, "that leaves the murder of Doctor Jim Wilson to be solved. You're not looking well this afternoon, Peppy. A little peaky."

Peppy had remained standing quietly beside Jack during this conversation.

Spoken to, he focused slowly.

"Peppy has something to say," Jack said. "He wants your help, Dad."

Fletch looked at Peppy and waited.

Peppy swallowed but said nothing.

Jack said, "One morning, Chet went to the stables at dawn, saddled two horses and went for a ride with his father. Only one morning."

Fletch said, "I know."

"Sitting, talking with me in the woods, Doctor Radliegh said his children never rode horses with him; one morning, Chet did ride with him. I didn't have the sense to realize he was offering me a clue. I didn't have the sense to ask, 'Why?' "

Fletch asked, "Do I need to?"

"So Peppy could drive to Birmingham, Alabama, to pick up a canister of gas for Chet."

Peppy said, "I didn't know what it was. I didn't know what it was for. I didn't know it was gas that could kill someone. It had a long name. Chet wrote it down for me on a piece of paper. He had ordered the canister in my name, I only found that out after I got there."

"Do you still have that piece of paper?" Fletch asked. "The one on which Chet wrote down the name of the gas?"

"Yes. I found it when Jack told me Doctor Wilson had been gassed to death. I have it at the cottage."

"That's good," Fletch said. "Will you give evidence in court against Chet?"

"Yes, sir."

"Well," Fletch said. "You see? Chet has self-destructed, too. Just as Chet was able enough not to flunk his bar exam, he was smart enough not to write down the name of a lethal gas he had already ordered in his own handwriting and give it to Peppy. Yet he did so." He stood up. "And, sir, I guess that's all the help I can be."

"I thought you were waiting for Shana," Jack said. "Protecting—"

"Shana is standing behind you," Fletch said. "With a knife in her hand. She has been for some moments."

Jack turned around.

In the black shorts, white shirt, and sneakers she had been wearing all day, Shana stood silently. In her hand was any kitchen's largest carving knife.

Her coal-black hair was a little tousled.

Her very wide-set, coal-black eyes were staring, but seemingly at nothing present, something in the middle distance, perhaps within herself.

"I think she would like you to take the knife from her, Jack," Fletch said. "Ms. Shana came here to do something. Listening to us talk, first from outside the door, she has come into the room slowly and quietly. And I don't think she any longer intends to do whatever she came here to do."

Jack took the knife from Shana's hand easily.

"I'm sorry to have involved you, Jack," Shana

said. "This is your father? Why is it . . . ?"

Jack asked, "Why is what?"

Never, ever did Shana Staufel speak again, not to police, defense attorneys, therapists, the courts, not to those who fed her and cared for her where she was institutionalized.

Not ever.

27

"Where do I put my suitcase?" With perplexity, Fletch studied Jack's blue Miata convertible.

Fletch had asked Jack to meet him at the front door of Vindemia's main house at four o'clock, to give him a lift.

"What are you doing with that big suitcase?" Jack asked from the driver's seat.

"Had to bring formal clothes, didn't I?"

Jack's duffel bag was stuffed in the little space behind the seats. He had thought there would be room for another.

When Jack had driven the two-seater under the oriole, many people were milling around in front of the house, going in and out. There were police in uniforms; police not in uniforms. There were newspaper reporters; television reporters and camera crews. Behind them all, Peppy stood alone, leaning his back against a wall, drinking lazily from a quart bottle of beer.

"You might just as well have brought your damned bicycle to pick me up," Fletch said standing over the passenger side of the car.

"You had your meeting with Lieutenant Corso?" Jack asked. "Everything is understood?"

"Yes." Still holding his suitcase, Fletch stepped down into the car. "I think I safely can say Corso understands the simple facts. Even that took hours."

Jack waved at Peppy.

Peppy gave a low wave back.

"Jack! Jack Faoni!" A television reporter Jack recognized only somewhat came to Jack's side of the car. "What are you doing here? If you're here, why am I here?"

"Beats me," Jack said.

"Are you on assignment?" the reporter asked. "For whom?"

"Global Cable News."

"Oh, no," said Jack.

"You work for Global Cable News. I had lunch at the same table with you last week in GCN's cafeteria in Virginia."

"Oh, yes," said Jack.

"You were working on the Tribal Nation story."

"I remember," said Jack.

"So are you covering the Radliegh story, or not?"

"Not," said Jack. "I don't work for GCN."

"You were last week."

"Oh, no." Jack put the car in gear. "I work for the truth."

Slowly he drove the little car around the groups of people in the semicircular driveway.

"Humph," Fletch said. "Good line."

Jack looked at his father.

Fletch sat in the passenger seat of the little car. The back of the suitcase was on his head. The front rested on the windshield frame.

Jack said, "I really don't think it's going to rain."

"Never can tell," Fletch said easily. Then, with more vigor, he said, "You can tell me where else I'm supposed to put it!"

"Don't ask!" Jack snapped.

At the end of the semicircular driveway, Fletch said, "Left. To the airstrip."

"The airstrip?"

"You expect me to ride all the way to Tennessee with a suitcase on my head?"

"Do you have an airplane waiting for you?"

"Yes."

"Oh." Jack turned left.

Fletch said, "You have more background, understanding of this story than anyone else."

"Right," Jack said.

"You're a reporter. You ought to report it."

"Right," Jack said.

"I mean, you could have called Andy Cyst. Even Alex Blair."

"Oh, no," Jack said.

"Why not?"

"I didn't let GCN in on the story early enough. What I learned from Mister Blair is that I should have called the television crew in as soon as I knew I was investigating this matter. You know, have them around to film Doctor Radliegh discovering the rigged coffeepot, the cabin exploding, the horse falling over dead on him at dawn, me and Alixis in bed, maybe even me and Shana in bed a few years ago in Stowe, Vermont. . . . Mrs. Radliegh hanging by the neck from a bedsheet tied to the balcony railing . . . all that good stuff . . . you know, getting as much of the story on film as possible. Do you think all that might have affected the story in any way? Anyway, Mister Blair explained to me that's the professional way to do a story, the way I'd have to do things to work for GCN."

"Oh, shut up."

"People who ride in cars wearing suitcases on their heads might just be more polite to whoever is driving. One pothole, and you'll want an aspirin."

"So what are you going to do with this story? Just throw it away? The public has a right to—"

"No."

"That's what I was going to say."

"I just faxed a complete report to Jack Saunders." Both his father, I. M. Fletcher, and his mother, Crystal Faoni, had worked with Jack Saunders on the *Boston Star*. Jack Saunders, now retired but far from inactive, also had befriended Jack while a student in Boston. Jack Faoni said, "Ol' Jack already has sold the story to an international newspaper syndicate. For a good price, too. He's editing it even as you ride through the Georgia countryside with a suitcase on your head."

"Print journalism?" Fletch smiled.

"Mister Blair can read all about it with the rest of the world in the morning newspapers," Jack said. "I shall refuse all interviews."

"I'll be . . ." Fletch said.

"I hope so." Jack stopped the car at the edge of the airstrip. "Now what? Do you wait for a plane to pick you up?"

"That yellow two-seater," Fletch said.

"What about it?"

"Will you drive me to it, please?"

"Why?"

"That's where I'm going."

"Oh, no. That airplane hasn't anything to do with you, has it?"

"Certainly."

"What?"

"I own it," Fletch said. "Bought and paid for."

"You don't fly it, do you?"

"That's the way it works," Fletch said. "I go up one place, down in another."

"Not possible."

"It got me here, didn't it? I wanted to see that Bierstadt. By the way, it's a wonderful painting. Flying in, I even watched you pedaling your bicycle along the road. Earthling."

"Where did you get an airplane like that?"

Slowly, Jack drove Fletch toward the airplane. "The Smithsonian? Don't they miss it?"

"I bought it from a friend. He needed the money."

"And you learned to fly it?"

"Not really. I use a road map and stay out of traffic."

"I didn't see it on the farm."

"I keep it in a shed."

"Who takes care of it for you?"

"Emory."

"Your farmhand? What does he know about airplanes? He can't even plug the muffler on his truck!"

"True, he's never been up in an airplane. Doesn't trust them. But he's very good with old engines. And regarding his truck muffler, I don't encourage him to fix it. I like to know when he leaves for lunch."

"Dad!" Jack stopped the car a few meters from the airplane. "That's a piece of junk!"

"It's a classic."

"It's very old. Very, very old."

"Yes," Fletch said. "It's a very old classic."

Fletch opened the car door and struggled to stand up with his suitcase. "Hasn't crashed yet. Well, yes it has. Not fatally, though. I mean, not fatally for the airplane."

He stepped up onto the wing, slid back the cockpit cover, and slipped his suitcase behind the two seats. "And my suitcase fits in it!"

Jack stood on the runway. "I'm just getting to know you. I can't let you go up in that . . . classic."

"Sure you can." Fletch stepped into the cockpit and fastened his safety belt. "Old dog leash." Fletch showed Jack one end of it, the end that usually attaches to a dog's collar. "Works perfectly well."

He cranked the engine twice.

"Damned thing doesn't even start," Jack said.

"Sure it does. Just needs a bit of encouragement." He cranked the engine again. "Sometimes it's a bit slow." Twice again. "Give it a push, will you?"

"Push the airplane?" Jack asked. "How?"

"Get behind and push." Fletch made a pushing motion with his hands.

Jack leaned his shoulders against the rudders and almost fell over. "This thing doesn't weigh twenty pounds!" he shouted. "Even with you in it!"

"Ah, yes," Fletch said. "She defies gravity, all right. Just watch her take off."

"If you can get the damned thing started," Jack muttered. With arms extended he pushed the airplane another ten meters.

With a great exhalation of exhaust smoke, the engine roared.

Fletch braked.

He yelled at Jack, "Will I see you back at the farm?"

Standing near the airplane he had pushed to get

started, listening to it, studying it, seeing it shuddering and flapping, Jack yelled, "I sincerely doubt it!"

Fletch chopped the air with his left hand. "Bye."